SECRET WILDERNESS SURVIVAL SKILLS FOR KIDS

A Hands-On Guide to Safe Outdoor Fun, Wildlife Knowledge, Ultimate Preparedness and Successful Adventures for Any Young Explorer.

BROOKS WILDLING

Table of Contents

Introduction

Imagine you're out in the wild, surrounded by nature's beauty and mystery, with only your wits and a few essential tools. The birds are chirping, the leaves rustling, and the sun shines through the trees. Now, what do you do next? This book is your ultimate guide to becoming a young wilderness explorer, packed with fun, practical survival skills you can use on your next adventure.

Mastering the art of navigating the wilderness, finding food and water, building shelters, and staying safe can transform any outdoor trip into an exhilarating, confidence-boosting adventure. Whether hiking with your family, camping with friends, or simply exploring your backyard, these skills will instill a sense of empowerment and make you feel like a true adventurer, ready to take on any challenge.

Each chapter begins with a short adventure story featuring our young explorers. These stories will show you the skills you'll learn in action.

This book is not just about reading—it's about doing! You'll find quizzes, scenarios, and projects designed to help you practice and master each skill. These activities are not just for fun; they are tools to reinforce your learning and test your understanding. For example, you might find a quiz on identifying animal tracks, a scenario where you must decide the best way to find water, or a project to build your mini shelter at home. These activities will make learning fun and engaging, sparking your curiosity and eagerness to learn more.

Safety is our top priority. Always remember to ask an adult for help when trying out these skills, and look out for our safety tips throughout the book. For example, if you're learning to start a fire, be sure an adult is with you. If you're practicing building a shelter, make sure you're in a safe area. These tips will keep you safe and secure while you learn and explore.

Prepare to embark on a journey that will spark your imagination, challenge your problem-solving skills, and build your confidence as a young explorer. You might imagine what you would do if you got lost in the woods, how you would find food if you were stranded, or even how you would signal for help if you were injured. These scenarios will help you think creatively and develop critical problem-solving skills.

As your guide, I bring my lifelong passion for the outdoors and the joy of sharing these experiences with my children. My name is Brooks Wilding, and from an early age, I've spent my life pursuing new adventures, hiking trails, and horseback riding. I got my first horse when I was only 4, and I've always had a talent for transforming the great outdoors into an exhilarating playground. Raised beneath the stars, I've enjoyed stargazing before I could even spell "constellation." From trekking Arizona's trails to enjoying cozy campfires, I've dedicated countless days and nights to exploring the wilderness. But my absolute joy is sharing these incredible experiences with my two children, who have grown up as true outdoor enthusiasts. From family hikes to stargazing adventures, I love seeing my kids—and all young adventurers—discover the magic of nature and feel that rush of confidence when they tackle a new challenge. So, grab your gear and prepare for an adventure—I'm here to show you how it's done!

1

The Adventure Begins

Have you ever wondered what it would be like to stumble upon a hidden treasure map while exploring the woods with your friends? Think about the excitement of finding clues, solving puzzles, and working together to uncover a hidden secret. Welcome to the world of the Wilderness Explorers, a group of kids like you who are about to embark on their first great adventure. The Wilderness Explorers is a club formed by Emily, Jack, Mia, and Sam, four brave young explorers who share a passion for the outdoors and a thirst for adventure. This chapter will introduce you to them and their unique skills and set the stage for their adventures in the wild.

1.1 Meeting the Wilderness Explorers

Let's get to know the main characters of our adventure, as they will be your guides and companions throughout the book. First up, we have Emily, the nature enthusiast. Emily has always had a special bond with the natural world. She can identify plants and animals with just a glance, and her pockets are always filled with interesting leaves, rocks, and sometimes even a bug or two! Emily's knowledge of nature is vast, and her curiosity is endless. She loves to share her discoveries with her friends, teaching them about the wonders of the wilderness.

Next, we have Jack, the curious problem-solver. Jack is the kind of kid who can fix just about anything with a piece of string and a paperclip. He loves gadgets and tools, and his backpack is always packed with all sorts of useful items. Jack's mind is like a puzzle, always working to figure out the best solution to any problem. His friends know they can count on him to come up with a clever plan when they find themselves in a tricky situation.

Mia, the safety-conscious leader, is the glue that holds the group together. She is meticulous, always thinking ahead and making sure everyone stays safe. Mia has a keen eye for detail and a wealth of knowledge about first aid. She's the one who makes sure everyone has their gear packed and knows what to do in an emergency. Her calm and composed nature helps the group stay focused and confident, even when things get tough.

Lastly, we have Sam, the imaginative storyteller. Sam's ability to spin captivating tales is unmatched. He can turn a simple walk in the woods into an epic adventure with dragons, knights, and hidden treasures. Sam's stories inspire courage and ignite the imagination of his friends. His creative mind brings a sense of wonder and excitement to every adventure, making even the most ordinary day feel extraordinary.

The explorers are ready for their first big adventure. Picture a dense forest with towering trees that seem to touch the sky. The air is filled with the sounds of birds chirping and leaves rustling in the gentle breeze. Squirrels dart from tree to tree, and insects buzz busily around. In the heart of this forest lies a rustic campsite, complete with a campfire ring and a cozy log cabin. This is where the Wilderness Explorers meet to plan their next great adventure.

Emily, Jack, Mia, and Sam gather in their favorite camping area, discussing their plans for the day. Emily excitedly shows the group a beautiful flower she found earlier, while Jack tinkers with a new gadget he brought along. Mia carefully checks their supplies, making sure they have everything they need, and Sam entertains everyone with a thrilling story about a lost treasure hidden deep in the forest.

As the sun rises higher in the sky, the group notices something unusual. Sam spots an old, weathered map tucked under a rock near an old gnarly log. With wide eyes and pounding hearts, the explorers eagerly unfold the map, revealing a series of clues leading to a hidden treasure. Their eyes light up with excitement as they realize they are about to embark on their first real adventure.

The group quickly gets to work, dividing roles and planning their strategy. Emily, with her keen knowledge of plants and animals, takes the lead in navigating the forest. Jack, ever the problem-solver, examines the map for any hidden details or puzzles that need solving. Mia, always thinking ahead, ensures they have all the necessary supplies and first aid materials. Sam, with his vivid imagination, keeps everyone's spirits high with tales of the treasure they are about to find.

As they follow the first clue, the explorers trek deeper into the forest, their senses heightened by the thrill of the hunt. They encounter various challenges along the way, from crossing a babbling brook to deciphering cryptic symbols etched into the bark of ancient trees. Each obstacle brings them closer together, rein-forcing their trust in one another and their determination to succeed.

Interactive Activity: Create Your Own Treasure Map

Why not join the Wilderness Explorers by creating your own trea-sure map? Grab a piece of paper and some colored pencils. Draw a map of your backyard, a nearby park, or even your favorite hiking trail. Mark the location of a hidden "treasure" (it could be anything from a small toy to a special rock). Add some fun clues and challenges along the way. Then, invite your friends or family to follow your map and see if they can find the treasure. This activity will help you practice navigation and problem-solving skills.

Back in the forest, our explorers finally reach the spot marked by the last clue. They dig into the earth with bated breath, uncovering a small, weathered chest. Inside, they find not gold or jewels, but something even more valuable—a sense of accomplishment and the joy of having worked together to achieve their goal. They realize that the true treasure lies in the adventure itself and the memories they have created together.

As the sun begins to set, casting a warm glow over the forest, the Wilderness Explorers make their way back to camp. They gather around the campfire, sharing stories of their adventure and reflecting on the skills they have learned. Emily talks about the plants and animals they encountered, Jack explains the puzzles they solved, Mia recounts how they stayed safe and prepared, and Sam, of course, spins a great tale that makes everyone laugh.

Their first adventure has not only taught them valuable survival skills but also strengthened their bond as friends and explorers. They know that this is just the beginning, and many more adventures await them in the wilderness. With their newfound knowledge and confidence, they are ready to take on whatever challenges the wild may throw their way.

So, are you ready to join the Wilderness Explorers on their next adventure? Let's see what the wild has in store for you!

1.2 Packing Your Bug Out Bag

Picture this: You're standing at the edge of a dense forest, ready to dive into an adventure that could lead you anywhere. But before you take that first step, you need to be prepared. Packing a bug out bag is like gearing up for the ultimate quest. It's the first critical step in wilderness survival, ensuring all necessary supplies are within reach and you're ready for unexpected situations. Imagine if you decided to explore a mysterious cave and suddenly realized you forgot your flashlight. Not fun, right? A well-packed bug out bag will make sure you're always ready for whatever the wild throws your way.

Let's talk about what goes into this magical bag. First, you'll need a water bottle and some purification tablets or a filter. Staying hydrated is key; you never know when you'll stumble upon a crystal-clear stream that might need some purifying. Next, a basic first aid kit is a must. Think of it as your mini-doctor's office, ready to handle cuts, scrapes, and minor injuries. A multi-tool and flashlight are also crucial. The multi-tool is like having a Swiss Army knife on steroids, ready to tackle any challenge, from cutting rope to fixing gear. The flashlight? It's your beacon in the dark, illuminating the path and keeping the shadows at bay.

Now write down each item as you pack it. Check it off once it's in your bag. This way, you can be confident that you're fully prepared for your adventure.

Bug Out Bag Checklist

- Water bottle (or water bladder) containing several ounces or liters of water)
- Purification tablets or filter
- Basic first aid kit (including mole skin)
- Multi-tool (including a small knife)
- A whistle
- Flashlight
- Snacks and lightweight food
- Map and compass
- Warm clothes
- Waterproof jacket
- Base layers
- Foil blanket
- Cord or rope (at least 6 ft)
- Emergency snacks (dried fruit, energy bars, mixed nuts)
- Waterproof matches, flint, and steel (or a couple of BIC lighters)
- Insect repellent
- Magnifying glass to use for starting a fire
- Small mirror (to use for signaling purposes if lost)
- Small roll of TP and small hand sanitizer container
- Dental floss
- Safety pins
- Cotton balls
- Superglue

As you pack your bag, think about the adventures that await you. Imagine navigating through dense forests, crossing streams, and setting up camp under the stars. Your bug out bag is your lifeline, your trusty companion in the wilderness. Each item you pack has a purpose and a story, ready to support you in your quest.

Remember, being prepared is more than just about having the right gear. It's about knowing how to use it and being ready for anything. Your bug-out bag is more than just a collection of items; it symbolizes your readiness, courage, and spirit of adventure. So pack it well, carry it with pride, and confidently step into the wild. The wilderness is calling, and you're ready to answer. You can't go exploring on an empty stomach. Pack some snacks and lightweight food. Dried fruit, energy bars, and mixed nuts are perfect for keeping your energy up without weighing you down. A map and compass are your best friends in the wild, helping you navigate and find your way back to camp. Remember to pack warm clothes, a waterproof jacket, base layers, and a foil blanket. Weather can be unpredictable, and staying warm and dry is crucial for survival. A cord or rope at least 6 feet long is another handy item. You can use it to build shelters, secure gear, or make a makeshift clothesline.

One thing you might not think of is dental floss. It's strong, lightweight, and can be used for everything from sewing up gear to fishing. Safety pins are another small but mighty item. They can fix torn clothes, hold bandages in place, or even act as makeshift hooks. Cotton balls soaked in petroleum jelly make excellent fire starters, and superglue can be a lifesaver for quick fixes. Imagine you're deep in the forest, and your shoe suddenly falls apart. A dab of super-glue, and you're back on track.

Packing your bug out bag efficiently is an art form. You don't want it to be too heavy, but you must also ensure you have everything you need. Start by distributing the weight evenly. Place heavier items at the bottom and closer to your back. This will help keep your balance and prevent the bag from feeling like a burden. Use compartments for easy access to your items. Keep things like your first aid kit and snacks in outer pockets, so you don't have to dig through your bag when you need them. Ensure comfort with padded straps. A bug out bag should feel like an extension of you, not a cumbersome load.

Here's where the fun part comes in: personalization. Adding a personal touch to your bug out bag makes it feel truly yours. Attach a keychain or patch that represents your personality. Maybe it's a mini-compass, a favorite character, or a symbol of your favorite hobby. Include a small toy or keepsake that brings you comfort. It could be a tiny stuffed animal, a family photo, or a lucky charm. These small touches make your bug out bag not just a piece of survival gear but a part of you.

To make this even more engaging, let's add an interactive element. How about a checklist to make sure you've packed everything you need? Grab a piece of paper and let's make a list!

1.3 Safety First – Always Ask an Adult!

When it comes to exploring the wilderness, safety should always be your top priority. The great outdoors is full of wonder, but it can also present challenges and dangers. That's why it's essential to understand safety protocols and always seek adult supervision when attempting survival skills. Imagine building a campfire for the first time without an adult. You might end up with more than just roasted marshmallows! Clear rules about when to ask for help are crucial. If you need clarification on a situation or a skill, feel free to contact an adult. Venturing out alone is never a good idea. Always have a buddy or an adult with you. If something goes wrong, you'll have someone there to help. And always tell someone at home where you are hiking (what trail or area), and approximately when you will return.

2

Navigating the Wild

I magine you're deep in the forest, where every tree looks the same, and the path seems to disappear into the shadows. How do you find your way back to camp? Navigation skills are like a secret map that helps you turn the confusing wilderness into a manageable playground. Our Wilderness Explorers, Emily, Jack, Mia, and Sam, are about to learn just how powerful these skills can be. As the sun rises and the morning mist begins to lift, the team prepares for a hike that will test their ability to navigate the wild.

The morning starts with excitement as the explorers pack their essentials and get ready to venture deeper into the forest. Emily checks her plant guide, Jack checks on his gadgets, Mia ensures everyone has their safety gear, and Sam spins a story about ancient explorers who never got lost. With backpacks secure and spirits high, they head out, eager to find new trails and hidden spots. However, halfway through their hike, they realize the path has become less distinct, and familiar landmarks are nowhere to be seen. It's time for some navigation skills!

Jack pulls out his compass, a small but mighty tool that can point the way when all else fails. He explains to the group how to take a bearing, a method used to determine direction. Holding the compass flat and stable, Jack aligns the needle with the orienting arrow, setting their course toward the campsite. The explorers start walking but soon encounter a fallen tree blocking their path. They adjust their route, using the compass to stay on track despite the obstacle

Emily takes out the map, a detailed forest drawing with trails, streams, and landmarks marked clearly. She points out key features they need to look for, like a large boulder shaped like a bear and a winding stream. Measuring the distance to the next waypoint, she calculates how far they need to go before changing direction. With the map and compass working together, they confidently navigate through the dense underbrush.

As they move deeper into the forest, they face a new challenge: the compass stops working due to interference from a large rock formation. But our explorers are prepared.

Mia suggests using natural navigation methods, starting with the sun. They know that the sun rises in the east and sets in the west, so they use its position to maintain their direction. They also recognize a distinctive rock formation that looks like a giant turtle, which they remember is close to their camp.

The explorers continue, using the sun and landmarks to guide them. Sam entertains everyone with tales of explorers who used stars to find their way at night. Luckily, they don't need to wait for nightfall to find their camp. As they follow the stream, they spot the familiar log cabin in the distance. Their navigation skills have led them back safely, turning what could have been a stressful situation into a triumphant return.

2.1 Reading a Compass - Finding Your Way

Imagine you're deep in the woods, trying to return to camp. The trees look the same, and the path has disappeared. What do you do? This is where a compass becomes your best friend. A compass is a small but powerful tool that helps you find your way when everything else seems confusing. It has three main parts: the needle, the baseplate, and the rotating bezel. The needle always points north, no matter which way you turn. This little gadget can guide you through forests, mountains, and open fields.

Using a compass might initially seem tricky, but it's really simple once you get the hang of it. First, you need to learn how to hold it properly. Keep the compass flat and stable in your hand, ensuring the needle can move freely. Next, align the needle with the orienting arrow on the baseplate. This step is crucial because it sets your direction. Once the needle and arrow are aligned, rotate the bezel to set your desired direction. The direction of travel arrow on the baseplate will point you where you need to go. Follow this arrow, and you'll be on the right path.

While using a compass, it's important to ensure accurate readings. Avoid metal objects or electronics that can interfere with the needle. Double-check your directions regularly to ensure you're still on track. Always have a backup navigation method, like a map or natural signs, just in case your compass stops working. These tips will help you stay safe and confident while navigating the wild.

Interactive Exercise: Create a Navigation Challenge

Why not test your navigation skills just like our Wilderness Explorers? Create a mini-navigation challenge in your backyard or local park. Draw a simple map with key landmarks, like a big tree, a playground, or a bench. Mark a start and end point, and use a compass to set your direction. Place small treasures or clues along the way to make it even more exciting. Invite friends or family to join you and see who can navigate the course the fastest. This exercise will help you practice using a map and compass, and it's a fun way to spend time outdoors.

Navigating the wild requires tools, knowledge, and quick thinking. Whether using a compass, reading a map, or following the sun, these skills will help you confidently explore. So, grab your gear, gather your friends, and get ready to turn the wilderness into your personal adventure playground.

2.2 Using Natural Signs for Direction

Sometimes, you might find yourself in the wild without a compass. Don't worry, nature offers plenty of clues to help you find your way. Think of the sun and stars as your celestial guides and landmarks like mountains and rivers as your trusty trail markers. Observing patterns in vegetation and animal behavior can also provide valuable hints about direction.

When the sun is out, it can be a reliable friend. The sun rises in the east and sets in the west, so you can use its position to figure out your direction. In the morning, if the sun is on your right, you face north. If the sun is on your left in the afternoon, you're still facing north. You can create a simple shadow stick compass to get even more precise. Find a straight stick and plant it upright in the ground. Mark the tip of the shadow cast by the stick with a small rock. Wait about 15 minutes and mark the new position of the shadow's tip. Draw a line between the two marks, and you'll have an approximate east-west line. The first mark is west, and the second is east. Stand with the first mark on your left, and you'll be facing north.

When night falls, the stars take over as your navigators. The North Star, known as Polaris, is a reliable guide to finding the north. To locate it, first find the Big Dipper, a constellation that looks like a ladle. The two stars at the end of the Big Dipper's bowl point directly to the North Star. Unlike other stars, the North Star stays in the same spot all night, making it a perfect reference point. Once you find the North Star, you'll know which way is north, and you can navigate accordingly. This method has guided explorers for centuries and can guide you too.

In addition to celestial navigation, natural landmarks are invaluable. Rivers and streams usually flow downhill, often leading to larger bodies of water or human settlements. Following their flow can guide you to safety or familiar territory. Distinctive natural features like a uniquely shaped rock or a large, solitary tree can serve as reference points. These landmarks help you keep track of your location and direction. Moss growth can also be a clue. In the Northern Hemisphere, moss tends to grow more thickly on the north side of trees because it's shadier and damper. This is only sometimes foolproof, but it's a handy trick when other clues are scarce.

Watching animal behavior provides additional insights. Birds flying in a specific direction in the evening might be heading to their nests, which are often in the same general area. Animals like deer and rabbits create paths through the forest, often leading to water sources. Insects can also be indicators; ants, for instance, often build their nests on the south side of trees or rocks to catch more sunlight. These behaviors have evolved over time, making animals unwitting guides in the wilderness.

Imagine you're in a dense forest, and your compass is nowhere to be found. You remember that the sun sets directly behind the hill where your camp is situated. As the day progresses, the sun begins to dip behind that hill. Using this natural clue, you adjust your direction and head towards the setting sun. Along the way, you spot a stream and recall it flows near your campsite. Following the stream, you recognize a large boulder shaped like a turtle, a landmark you noted earlier. With these natural signs, you successfully navigate back to camp, proving that nature can be an excellent guide.

2.3 Creating Your Own Trail Markers

Imagine you're exploring the forest, and every tree starts to look the same. It's like being in a maze with no end in sight. This is where trail markers become your best friends. Creating trail markers is vital for navigation and safety. They help prevent you from getting lost by marking your path. If you need assistance, these markers can guide rescuers to your location. Plus, they leave a traceable route to return to your starting point. Think of them as breadcrumbs in a fairy tale, leading you safely back home.

There are several types of trail markers you can create using natural materials. Rock cairns are one of the simplest. Stack small rocks in a noticeable pile, and voilà, you have a marker that's hard to miss. Stick arrows are another great option. Arrange sticks on the ground to point in the direction you need to go. This method is quick and effective. Tree blazes are also handy. Make a small, noticeable mark on the bark of a tree. Just be gentle and ensure you're not harming the tree. These markers can be lifesavers, guiding you through the wild like a trusty map.

Creating trail markers is an art that requires a bit of practice. Start by choosing visible and durable materials. If your markers blend into the background, they will be little help. Place them at regular intervals and at key turning points. Imagine you're leaving clues for a treasure hunt. You want your friends to find the treasure, stay aware along the way. Ensure your markers are clear and easy to understand. A confusing marker is worse than no marker at all!

Interactive Activity: Create Your Own Trail Markers Challenge

Why not create a trail marker challenge to make this even more fun? Gather your friends or family and head to a safe, familiar area like a park or backyard. Split into teams and give each team a set of supplies to create trail markers. Set up a course with a starting point and a treasure at the end. Teams will place their trail markers along the course, leading to the treasure. Once everyone's done, swap courses and see if you can follow the other team's markers to find the treasure. This activity is exciting and helps you practice your trail-marking skills.

So, remember trail markers' power next time you're out exploring. They might seem like simple piles of rocks or sticks, but they can make a difference in navigating the wild. Happy marking!

2.4 Creating an Emergency Signal

Imagine you're out in the wilderness and suddenly realize you're lost. Panic begins to set in, but you remember the importance of staying calm and signaling for help. Emergency signals are crucial when you're lost or injured because they make it easier for rescuers to find you. Knowing how to create these signals can be the difference between being found quickly and spending hours—or even days—waiting for help. Let's explore some practical methods for creating emergency signals that can make you stand out in the vast expanse of nature.

One simplest yet most effective emergency signal is creating large ground signals using rocks or branches. Picture this: you're in an open area, gathering large rocks to spell out "SOS" or creating an arrow pointing in the direction you need help. These signals are easy to spot from the air and can guide rescuers directly to you. Always choose a visible location for your ground signals, like a clearing or an open field, where they can be seen clearly from above. Using contrasting colors, like white rocks on dark soil or green leaves on sand, makes your signals even more noticeable.

Another handy method is using a whistle to produce loud, distinct sounds. A whistle's sharp, piercing noise can be heard over long distances, cutting through the forest's rustling leaves and animal sounds. Three short blasts on a whistle are a universally recognized distress signal. Keep a whistle on a lanyard around your neck or attach it to your backpack for easy access. Practicing with your whistle ensures you know how to use it effectively in an emergency.

Reflecting sunlight with a mirror or shiny object is another powerful way to signal for help. When the sun is out, you can use a small mirror, a piece of foil, or even your phone screen to reflect sunlight and create a bright flash. Aim the reflected light at passing planes, helicopters, or distant hikers. The flash can travel great distances and catch the attention of rescuers. Practicing this technique beforehand will help you aim the light more accurately when needed.

Building a signal fire is another classic method. Adding green branches to the fire can create thick, white smoke that rises high into the air, visible from miles away. Choose a safe, open location for your signal fire, and make sure you have water or sand nearby to control the flames. Never leave a fire unattended; always extinguish it thoroughly after use to prevent wildfire. Signal fires are beneficial during the day when the smoke can be easily seen against the sky.

Now, let's put these skills to the test with an interactive activity. Find an open area where you can practice creating ground signals. Gather rocks, branches, or leaves, and design an "SOS" signal or an arrow pointing to your location. Next, practice using a whistle to produce three short blasts. Try reflecting sunlight using a mirror or any shiny object you have. Emergency signals are vital for ensuring your safety in the wilderness. By practicing these techniques and understanding the best practices for making your signals visible and effective, you'll be well-prepared for any situation. Remember to choose open, visible signal locations and use contrasting colors. These skills will boost your confidence and ensure you can get help when you need it most.

As we wrap up this chapter on navigating the wild, remember that these skills are your key to exploring the wilderness safely and confidently. Whether using a compass, following natural signs, creating trail markers, or signaling for help, each skill adds to your toolkit as a young explorer. Now that you're equipped with these essential navigation techniques, you're ready to move on to the next exciting adventure in your journey of wilderness survival.

3

Mastering Fire Making

P icture yourself deep in the forest, the air filled with the scent of pine and the sound of chirping birds. The sun is starting to dip below the horizon, and you and your friends are planning an overnight camping adventure on your treasure-hunting journey. But wait, what's an overnight adventure without a campfire to cook your food? This chapter is about mastering the art of fire-making, a skill that will keep you warm and make your food deliciously toasty. If planning to camp overnight there may be additional items to pack. For instance protective gloves if you are practicing the flint and steel method or perhaps a bucket to grab some water to help douse the fire.

The Wilderness Explorers, Emily, Jack, Mia, and Sam, had been following the treasure map they found earlier. After a long day of searching for clues and navigating through the forest, they decided to take a break and enjoy a well-deserved picnic. But first, they needed to start a campfire. Always prepared, Emily pulled out her flint and steel, while Jack, the innovator, grabbed his magnifying glass. The stage was set for a fire-starting showdown.

Emily crouched down, gathering some dry leaves and small twigs for tinder. She struck the flint against the steel, creating a shower of sparks. The sparks landed on the tinder, and after a few attempts, a small flame flickered to life. She carefully added more twigs and small sticks, nurturing the flame until it grew into a crackling fire. The look of triumph on her face was priceless.

Meanwhile, Jack was determined to show that his magnifying glass could do the job just as well. He positioned it at the right angle to focus the sunlight onto a piece of dry bark. The concentrated light created a tiny, glowing spot that began to smoke. With a bit of patience and a gentle blow, the smoldering bark burst into flames. Jack added more tinder and soon had his own fire blazing. The explorers cheered, impressed by their dual success.

With the fire roaring, it was time to cook their food. Mia had packed marshmallows and hot dogs, perfect for roasting over the flames. They found long, sturdy sticks and sharpened one end for skewers. Carefully, they threaded the hot dogs onto the sticks and held them over the fire. The hot dogs sizzled and popped, turning a delicious golden brown. Next came the marshmallows, which they toasted perfectly, with crispy, caramelized exteriors and gooey centers.

As they sat around the campfire, enjoying their meal, the explorers took a moment to reflect on the lessons they had learned. The importance of fire safety was evident. They kept a safe distance from the flames and had a bucket of water nearby, just in case. They also learned the value of patience and perseverance. Starting a fire with flint and steel or a magnifying glass wasn't easy, but with practice and determination, they succeeded. The reward of a warm, tasty meal made all their efforts worthwhile.

The explorers also discovered the joy of working together. Emily's expertise with flint and steel and Jack's ingenuity with the magnifying glass showed that there are multiple ways to achieve the same goal. Sharing their skills and knowledge made the experience even more enriching. They realized that teamwork and cooperation are as important as the skills themselves in the wilderness.

Interactive Activity: Fire Safety Quiz

Let's test your fire safety knowledge! Answer the following questions to see how well you understand the basics of fire safety.

1. What should you always have nearby when starting a fire?
   - A) A bucket of water
   - B) Extra sticks
   - C) A flashlight

2. Why is it important to keep a safe distance from the flames?
   - A) So you don't burn your food
   - B) To avoid getting too hot
   - C) To prevent burns and accidents

3. What is the first step in starting a fire with flint and steel?
   - A) Adding large logs
   - B) Striking the flint against the steel
   - C) Gathering dry leaves and small twigs

4. How do you use a magnifying glass to start a fire?
   - A) Position it to focus sunlight onto tinder
   - B) Use it to find dry wood
   - C) Shine it on a mirror

5. What should you do if the fire gets out of control?
   - A) Run away
   - B) Throw more sticks on it
   - C) Use water or sand to extinguish it

Answers: 1: A, 2: C, 3: C, 4: A, 5: C

So, as you plan your next adventure, remember the power of fire. It's not just about warmth; it's about cooking delicious food, creating a cozy atmosphere, and bringing friends together. With your newfound fire-making skills, you're ready to tackle the wilderness and enjoy the rewards of your efforts. Now, who's ready for some more marshmallows?

3.1 The Magic of Flint and Steel

Imagine holding the tools that ancient humans used to tame the wild: flint and steel. These are no ordinary rocks and metals. Flint is a type of hard quartz that creates sparks when struck against steel , a process that seems almost magical. The steel , often shaped like a small bar or striker, is designed to create friction when it makes contact with the flint. This friction produces tiny, glowing sparks that can ignite tinder and start a fire. Using flint and steel is like stepping back in time, connecting with the survival skills of our ancestors who relied on these simple tools to cook food, stay warm, and fend off wild animals.

To understand the magic behind flint and Steel, let's break it down. When you strike the Steel against the flint, tiny pieces of Steel are shaved off. The friction between the two materials heats these tiny pieces until they become sparks. These sparks are incredibly hot, reaching around 2,500 degrees Fahrenheit—hot enough to ignite Tinder. The process might seem simple, but it requires practice and precision. The angle of the strike, the force you use, and the quality of your materials all play crucial roles in creating those vital sparks.

Flint and Steel have a rich history in survival. Before matches and lighters were invented, people used these tools to start fires. Imagine early explorers and pioneers huddled around a campfire they started with flint and Steel, sharing stories and planning their next adventure. These tools were so reliable that they were carried in small tins or pouches, always ready for use. Today, flint and Steel are still prized by survivalists and outdoor enthusiasts for their reliability and the sense of connection they provide to our survivalist heritage.

Now that you know the basics, let's get hands-on. First, gather your materials. You'll need Tinder, kindling, and some dry leaves. Tinder is any material that catches fire quickly. Dry leaves, grass, or even cotton balls soaked in petroleum jelly work great. Kindling consists of small sticks and twigs that will catch fire from the Tinder and help build your fire. Once you have your materials, it's time to prepare your flint and Steel. Hold the flint in one hand and the steel striker in the other.

Hold the flint steady to create sparks and strike the Steel against it quickly and firmly. Aim the sparks toward your Tinder. It might take a few tries, but keep going. Once the sparks land on the Tinder, gently blow on it to help the flames grow. As the Tinder ignites, carefully add small twigs and sticks to build the fire. Gradually add larger logs to sustain the fire, ensuring it has enough airflow to keep burning.

Fire safety is paramount when using flint and Steel. Always wear protective gloves to prevent scrapes and burns. Make sure you're in a clear area free of flammable materials like dry grass or leaves. Practicing under adult supervision is essential, especially if you're new to fire starting. Keep a bucket of water or sand nearby to extinguish the fire if it gets out of control.

Remember, fire is a powerful tool, and respecting it is crucial for your safety and the safety of those around you.

The magic of flint and steel lies not just in their ability to create fire, but in the sense of accomplishment and connection to history they bring. As you master this skill, you'll feel a part of a long lineage of explorers and survivalists who relied on these simple yet powerful tools. So gather your materials, strike your steel, and watch as sparks turn into flames, lighting up your wilderness adventures.

3.2 Using a Magnifying Glass to Ignite a Fire

Picture yourself in a sunny clearing, the warmth of the sun on your face and a magnifying glass in your hand. Believe it or not, that magnifying glass isn't just for making ants look like monsters. It's a powerful tool for starting a fire, using nothing but sunlight. The science behind it is pretty cool. When you hold a magnifying glass up to the sun, it focuses the light into a tiny, intense spot. This focused light creates heat, which can get hot enough to ignite tinder.

To make this work, you need strong, direct sunlight. Cloudy days won't cut it, and you might end up just waving a magnifying glass around like a wizard without a wand. Historically, magnifying glasses have been used for everything from lighting fires to studying insects up close. Ancient civilizations even used polished crystals to achieve a similar effect, showing that humans have long known how to harness the power of the sun.

Ready to give it a try? First, you need to choose the right tinder. Dry leaves, grass, or even small pieces of bark work well. You want something that catches fire easily, so avoid anything damp or too thick. Place your tinder in a small pile where it won't blow away. Next, hold the magnifying glass between the sun and the tinder, adjusting the angle until the light focuses into a small, bright spot. It's like playing with a laser beam, but without the batteries. Move the magnifying glass slowly until you see the spot start to smolder.

Keep the focused light steady on the tinder, and with a bit of patience, you'll see a tiny wisp of smoke. That's your cue to gently blow on the tinder, feeding it oxygen to encourage the flames. Once it catches, add small twigs and sticks to build up your fire, just like you learned before. It's a method that requires a bit of finesse, but mastering it can make you feel like a true wilderness champion.

When using a magnifying glass to start a fire, safety is super important. First, never look directly at the focused light. It can be as intense as staring at the sun, and you don't want to fry your eyeballs. Make sure you keep a safe distance from the fire as it grows. Fire can be unpredictable, and you don't want any surprises. Always have water or a fire extinguisher nearby, so you can put out the fire if it gets out of control. Practicing under adult supervision is a must.

Imagine the thrill of seeing those tiny sparks turn into flames, knowing you did it all with just sunlight and a magnifying glass. It's a skill that not only connects you with ancient practices but also adds a touch of magic to your wilderness adventures. So, grab your magnifying glass, find a sunny spot, and let the power of the sun light up your wild explorations.

3.3 Maintaining Your Campfire

Imagine you've just successfully started a fire, and the warm glow is lighting up the evening. But starting a fire is just the beginning. Maintaining it is the key to keeping warm, cooking your food, and ensuring you don't end up with a wildfire on your hands. Fire maintenance is crucial for both safety and efficiency. If you let your fire get out of control, it can spread quickly, causing a dangerous situation. On the other hand, if you don't keep it fed, it might just fizzle out, leaving you cold and hungry.

One of the first things you need to understand is how to properly add fuel to keep the fire burning. It's not as simple as throwing a huge log onto the flames and calling it a day. Start by adding small sticks and branches gradually. These smaller pieces catch fire more easily and help build a strong base of coals. Once the fire is going strong, you can add larger logs, but even then, you need to ensure they're placed in a way that allows for good airflow. Fire needs oxygen to burn, so you don't want to smother it by piling on too much wood at once.

Ensuring the fire stays lit is an ongoing task. You can't just light it and walk away. It is imperative that you keep an eye on it, adding fuel as needed and making sure it doesn't get too big or too small. If the flames die down, add smaller sticks to reignite it. If it's roaring too fiercely, you might need to move some logs aside to reduce its intensity. Think of it like tending a garden; a little attention goes a long way in keeping things healthy and thriving.

Fire control techniques are essential for managing the size and intensity of your fire. For example, if you want a small, controlled fire for cooking, arrange the logs in a teepee shape. This allows the flames to rise and concentrate in the center, perfect for roasting marshmallows or cooking hot dogs. If you need a larger fire for warmth, spread the logs out in a crisscross pattern. This creates a wider base and more surface area for the wood to burn, producing more heat.

Another important aspect of fire maintenance is knowing when and how to put it out. Never leave a fire unattended, even for a short time. If you need to leave, make sure you extinguish the fire completely. Pour water over the flames, stirring the ashes to ensure all the embers are out. If you don't have water, use sand or dirt. Cover the fire with a thick layer and mix it in until no glowing embers are left. This step is crucial for preventing forest fires and keeping the wilderness safe for everyone.

Maintaining a campfire is like a dance between you and the elements. You need to be in tune with the fire's needs, feeding it just the right amount of fuel and keeping an eye on its behavior. It's a skill that takes practice, but once you get the hang of it, you'll feel like a true wilderness expert. Plus, there's nothing quite like the satisfaction of sitting around a well-maintained fire, its warmth and light creating a cozy atmosphere in the great outdoors.

As the flames flicker and crackle, you'll realize that maintaining a campfire is more than just a practical skill. It's an art form, a way to connect with nature and enjoy the simple pleasures of outdoor life. So next time you're out in the wild, remember to respect the fire, tend to it with care, and enjoy the warmth and comfort it brings.

With these fire maintenance skills in your toolkit, you're ready to confidently explore the wilderness. Whether you're cooking a meal, staying warm, or simply enjoying the ambiance, knowing how to keep your fire under control will make all the difference in your outdoor adventures.

4

Finding and Purifying Water

Visualize you're on a thrilling adventure with your friends, deep in the wilderness, and suddenly you realize something critical—you're out of water! The sun is blazing, and your water bottles are empty. You feel like an explorer in a desert, desperate for a sip of water. But don't worry; this is where your survival skills kick in. You gather your friends, and together, you use your wits to find a water source and purify it for drinking and cooking. This chapter will guide you through the exciting process of locating and purifying water, just like our Wilderness Explorers.

4.1 The Explorers Locate and Purify Water!!

The Wilderness Explorers had a fantastic time following the trea-sure map they had found earlier. They had navigated through dense forests, climbed over rocky terrain, and even built a cozy shelter for the night. But as they prepared for dinner, they realized they had a big problem—they were out of water. Their canteens were bone dry, and the nearest stream they had seen was miles away.

"We can't cook or drink without water," said Mia, looking concerned.

"Don't panic," Jack said, always the problem-solver. "We just need to find a new water source. Let's think about where water might be." The group gathered around, brainstorming ideas. They knew water often collects in low-lying areas, so they headed downhill. As they walked, they kept their eyes peeled for signs of water—green vegetation, animal tracks, and damp soil.

After a short hike, they stumbled upon a small, muddy puddle. "This might be a good sign," said Emily, examining the area. "But we need something cleaner." They followed a narrow trail that led them to a small stream, its water glistening in the sunlight. They cheered, excited to have found a potential water source. But they knew they couldn't drink it straight from the stream. It needed to be purified first.

"Remember what we learned about purification?" asked Sam, pulling out their gear. "We have a few methods in our bags." The explorers had packed purification tablets, a small portable filter, and even a metal pot for boiling water if necessary. They decided to try the tablets first. Jack carefully read the instructions on the package. "It says we need one tablet per liter of water. We have enough for all our canteens."

They filled their water bottles with the stream water, avoiding any floating debris. Jack dropped a tablet into each one and shook them vigorously. "Now we wait for the tablets to do their magic," he said. The instructions indicated they needed to wait at least 30 minutes before the water was safe to drink. While they waited, they gathered around the campfire they had built earlier, sharing stories and keeping their spirits high. Finally, the moment of truth arrived. Mia took a cautious sip from her canteen. "It tastes fine," she said, smiling. The others followed suit, relieved to have clean, safe water. They used the purified water to cook their dinner, enjoying a warm meal under the stars. The experience taught them the importance of staying hydrated and being prepared with multiple water purification methods.

As they sat around the campfire, they reflected on their adventure. They navigated the wilderness, built a shelter, and successfully found and purified water. Their confidence grew with each challenge they overcame, knowing they could rely on their survival *skills. The Wilderness Explorers were ready for whatever the wild had in store for them next.*

4.2 Finding Water Sources in Nature

You're deep in the wilderness, and your throat feels as dry as a desert. What do you do? Finding water in nature is like playing detective; the clues are all around you. Let's start with the most obvious sources: streams and rivers. Flowing water is usually a reliable find. It's constantly moving, which helps keep it clean. Look for areas where the land dips, like valleys or canyons, and follow the sound of rushing water. If you spot a stream, you've hit the jackpot. But remember, even flowing water can contain contaminants, so you'll need to purify it before drinking.

Lakes and ponds can also be good sources, but they're trickier. Standing water doesn't move, which means it's more likely to host bacteria and other nasties. Look for signs of life around the water. If you see fish or birds, that's a good sign. However, always take extra precautions to purify this water. Rainwater collection is another nifty trick. Nature provides plenty of ways to gather rainwater. Natural depressions in rocks or the ground can act as mini reservoirs. You can also use large leaves to funnel rain into containers. It's like setting up a water trap, and Mother Nature does all the work for you.

Now, let's talk about the signs that water is nearby. Green vegetation is a big clue. Lush, green plants often indicate a water source underground. Think of it like a green neon sign saying, "Water here!" Follow the greenest plants, like ferns, or trees to find hidden water.

Animal tracks are another excellent indicator. Animals need water just like we do, and they'll often lead you to it. Look for well-trodden paths or clusters of tracks in the mud. These animal highways usually end at a water source.

Damp soil and mud are also promising signs. Water is likely close to the surface if the ground squelches under your feet. Dig a little, and you might find a small pool of water. Speaking of digging, let's explore techniques for finding underground water. In dry riverbeds, moisture can still be present beneath the surface. Digging into the sand or gravel can reveal hidden water. It's like finding buried treasure, except this treasure keeps you hydrated.

Natural rock formations can also be your ally. Water often seeps from rocks, collecting in small crevices. Look for areas where the rock feels damp or where moss is growing. Use a container to collect the water slowly dripping from these spots. It's a bit like milking a stone, but every drop counts.

Safety and hygiene are crucial when dealing with natural water sources. Stagnant water is a no-go. It's a breeding ground for bacteria and parasites. Always ensure the water is flowing or freshly collected. Before drinking, check the water for clarity and odor. Clear water is usually better, but clarity alone isn't a guarantee of safety. Always purify water before drinking it. You can use boiling, purification tablets, or filters to ensure it's safe.

Finding water in nature is an adventure in itself. With these tips and techniques, you'll be well-prepared to quench your thirst and stay hydrated on your wilderness explorations. Happy water hunting!

4.3 Boiling Water for Safety

Think about being in the middle of the woods, and you've just found a sparkling stream. The water looks clear, but you know that looks can be deceiving. This is where understanding the science of boiling water becomes a lifesaver. When you boil water, the heat kills harmful microorganisms like bacteria, viruses, and parasites. These tiny creatures can cause all sorts of nasty illnesses if ingested. Boiling water works because the high temperature disrupts the cell structures of these microorganisms, effectively neutralizing them.

The boiling point of water is 212 degrees Fahrenheit (100 degrees Celsius) at sea level. To effectively purify water, you need to bring it to a rolling boil, where bubbles vigorously rise from the bottom to the top. Keep it boiling for at least one minute. If you're at a higher altitude, say above 6,500 feet, you should let it boil for three minutes because water boils at a lower temperature in thinner air.

Now, let's get into the nitty-gritty of how to boil water in the wilderness. First, gather your materials: a pot or container and a reliable fire source. Your pot can be anything that

holds water and can withstand heat, like a metal container or a traditional camping pot. If you don't have a pot, don't worry—I'll cover some alternative methods later.

Next, you'll need to start a controlled fire using the fire-making skills you've learned. Whether you're using flint and steel or a magnifying glass, get that fire going. Once the fire is stable, place your pot filled with water over the flames. Keep an eye on it, making sure it reaches a rolling boil. The water should be bubbling vigorously, not just simmering.

This ensures that the temperature is high enough to kill any harmful microorganisms.

But what if you don't have a traditional pot? Fear not! You can use other metal containers like empty cans. Wash them out thoroughly before using them to boil water. If metal containers are unavailable, you can improvise with materials like tin foil or even heated rocks. Wrap the tin foil into a bowl, fill it with water, then place it carefully near the fire. For heated rocks, place clean stones in the fire until they're hot, then drop them into a water container. The heat from the rocks will cause the water to boil, though this method requires more time and patience.

Safety is paramount when boiling water. Avoid burns by using proper tools like tongs or thick gloves to handle hot containers. Never touch a hot pot with bare hands; it's a surefire way to get burned. Ensure your fire is controlled and safe, free from flammable materials. Always have water or sand nearby to extinguish the fire if it gets out of control. Keep a close watch on the boiling process to prevent the pot from tipping over or the fire from spreading.

To make this even more interactive, let's try a quick exercise. Imagine you're out camping with your family, and it's your job to boil water for everyone. First, gather your materials— a pot, water, and fire-making tools. Start your fire and place the pot on it. Monitor the boiling process, making sure the water reaches a rolling boil and stays boiling for at least one minute. Once done, carefully remove the pot using tongs or thick gloves. Let it cool, and then enjoy your safe, purified water.

Boiling water might seem simple, but it's a crucial skill in wilderness survival. It ensures you stay hydrated without risking your health. So, next time you're out in the wild and need a drink, remember the power of boiling water and the science that makes it work.

4.4 Using Purification Tablets and Filters

Imagine you're on a hike with your friends, and you come across a crystal-clear stream. The water looks tempting, but you know better than drinking it from the source. This is where purification tablets and filters come into play. Purification tablets are tiny, powerful tablets that use chemicals like chlorine or iodine to kill harmful microorganisms in the water. These chemicals break down the cell walls of bacteria, viruses, and parasites, rendering them harmless. Different types of tablets are available, each with its specific instructions, so it's essential to know how to use them properly.

To get started with purification tablets, first read the instructions carefully. Each type of tablet has its own guidelines, and it's crucial to follow them to ensure the water is safe. Begin by calculating the dosage, typically one tablet per liter of water. If you're using a larger container, adjust the number of tablets accordingly. Drop the tablets into your water container, close the lid tightly, and shake it well to ensure they dissolve completely. Then, the waiting game begins. Most tablets require at least 30 minutes to work, but some may need up to four hours. Be patient and allow the chemicals to neutralize any harmful microorganisms in the water.

Let's talk about water filters while you're waiting for the tablets to work their magic. Filters are fantastic tools that remove impurities from water, making it safe to drink. There are several types of filters, each with its unique mechanism. Pump filters are famous for their efficiency. They manually pump water through a filter cartridge that traps bacteria, protozoa, and other contaminants. To use a pump filter, set up the device according to the manufacturer's instructions. Place the intake hose in the water source and start pumping. Clean water will flow out of the outlet hose and into your container.

Straw filters are another handy option. These portable devices allow you to drink directly from a water source, like a stream or lake, without needing a separate container. Place one end of the straw in the water and suck through the other end. The filter inside the straw removes harmful microorganisms as the water passes through. It's like drinking through a magic wand that turns dirty water into clean, drinkable water.

For larger groups or longer trips, gravity filters are a great choice. These filters use gravity to pull water through a filtration system, making them easy to use with minimal effort. To set up a gravity filter, fill the reservoir with water and hang it from a tree or another high point. Gravity will do the rest, pulling the water through the filter and into a clean container below. It's a hands-free way to get plenty of purified water.

To ensure your purification tablets and filters are effective, store them properly. Keep tablets dry and cool, and check expiration dates regularly. Filters need regular cleaning and maintenance to function correctly. Follow the manufactur-er's instructions for cleaning and replacing the filter cartridges when necessary. Before using any filter, test the water clarity. Remove any large particles or debris that could clog the filter. This extra step ensures your filter works efficiently and extends its lifespan.

Knowing how to use purification tablets and filters is vital for any young explorer. These tools provide safe drinking water, keeping you hydrated and healthy on your adventures. So, next time you're out in the wild and come across a tempting water source, remember the power of purification tablets and filters. With these skills, you can tackle any wilderness challenge and enjoy the great outdoors safely.

4.5 Homemade Water Filters

What if you're out in the wild and found a stream, but the water's murky and filled with tiny bits of debris. Drinking it straight would be like sipping from a muddy puddle. This is where homemade water filters come in handy. They help remove debris and some impurities, making drinking water safer. Think of it as giving the water a good scrub before purifying it.

The basic principle of water filtration is simple: you're using different layers of materials to trap dirt and particles. As water passes through the layers, each one catches different sizes of debris. By the time the water reaches the bottom, it's much cleaner. This method won't remove bacteria or viruses, but it's an excellent first step in making drinking water safer.

To create a homemade water filter, you'll need a few materials. Grab a plastic bottle or container, sand, gravel, and activated charcoal. You'll also need a piece of cloth or a coffee filter. These materials are easy to find and can be packed into your bug out bag. The plastic bottle acts as the body of the filter, while the sand, gravel, and charcoal each play a crucial role in trapping different impurities.

Now, let's build this filter step by step. First, take the plastic bottle and cut off the bottom. This will be the top of your filter where you'll pour the water. Next, place the piece of cloth or coffee filter inside the neck of the bottle. This will act as the first layer, catching the largest particles and preventing the smaller materials from falling out.

Next, add a layer of activated charcoal. Charcoal is excellent at absorbing impurities and removing odors. After the charcoal, add a layer of fine sand. Sand helps catch smaller particles that the charcoal might miss. On top of the sand, add a layer of gravel. Gravel traps larger debris and helps keep the sand in place. Finally, place another piece of cloth or coffee filter on top to keep everything from shifting around.

Now, you're ready to filter some water. Pour the murky water into the top of the bottle. Watch as it trickles through the layers, getting cleaner with each step. The water should be much clearer when it reaches the bottom. Collect the filtered water in a clean container. Remember, this water must still be purified to remove harmful microorganisms. Boil it or use purification tablets to ensure it's safe to drink.

Let's make this even more exciting with a practical activity. Gather the materials with adult supervision and build your own homemade water filter. Follow the steps carefully, and once your filter is ready, test it with some dirty water. Observe the results and note how much clearer the water becomes. This hands-on experience will help you understand the process and give you a valuable skill for your outdoor adventures.

Homemade water filters are a fantastic tool for any young explorer. They're easy to make, use simple materials, and provide an essential first step in water purification. By understanding and practicing this skill, you'll be better prepared for any situation where clean water is hard to find.

So, next time you're out in the wilderness and come across a murky stream, remember the power of homemade water filters. With a few simple materials and some know-how, you can turn muddy water into something much safer to drink. And you might even impress your friends with your DIY water purification skills.

5

Foraging for Food

You're on a thrilling adventure with your friends, and your stomach starts growling like a bear. You didn't pack enough snacks, but you're not worried. Why? Because you know how to find food in the wild! This chapter will teach you the fantastic skill of foraging, turning any wilderness trip into a delicious and exciting picnic. Our Wilderness Explorers are about to show you how it's done.

5.1 The Explorers Find Food!

The day was perfect for a picnic. Emily, Jack, Mia, and Sam set out with their backpacks, determined to gather dinner from the forest. They had learned about foraging and were excited to put their skills to the test. As they wandered deeper into the woods, the first thing they noticed was a patch of dandelions. Emily, the nature enthusiast, explained, "Dandelions are great because every part of them is edible. The leaves can be used in salads, the flowers can be fried, and the roots can be roasted." They carefully picked some dandelions, leaving enough for nature to thrive.

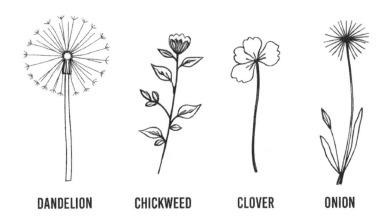

DANDELION   CHICKWEED   CLOVER   ONION

Next, they stumbled upon a field dotted with clover. Clover leaves are also edible," said Mia. "They can be added to salads or eaten raw." They gathered a handful of clover, their picnic basket slowly filling with nature's bounty. The excitement grew as they moved further into the woods, their eyes scanning the ground for more edible treasures.

The real treat came when they found a thicket of blackberry bushes. Sam, couldn't help but weave a tale about a hidden kingdom where the bushes guarded the entrance to a treasure-filled cave. While he spun his story, the others picked the ripe, juicy berries. "Blackberries are delicious and full of vitamins," Jack added, popping one into his mouth. The sweetness of the berries made all their efforts worth it.

Their adventure took a turn when they encountered some plants that looked suspiciously like Nightshade. Emily quickly identified them and warned, "Nightshade is toxic. We need to be careful and avoid these." They marked the spot on their map as a danger zone. This was a valuable lesson in recognizing and steering clear of harmful plants.

As they continued, the explorers faced another challenge—pesky insects. Mosquitoes buzzed around, making it hard to concentrate. Jack, ever the problem-solver, had a solution. "Let's use some of the wild mint we found earlier. Rubbing the leaves on our skin can help repel mosquitoes." They did just that, and the minty scent kept the bugs at bay, allowing them to focus on their foraging.

Finally, they reached a grove where wild raspberriess grew. The bright red berries were a delightful find. They carefully picked the raspberries, making sure not to disturb the plants too much. "Always take only what you need and leave some for the wildlife," Mia reminded them. They filled their baskets, and their picnic was now complete with a variety of greens and berries.

Interactive Activity: Foraging Journal

Why not start your own foraging journal? Grab a notebook and head out to a safe area with an adult. Note down the plants and berries you find, sketch their shapes and write about their uses. This activity will help you remember what you learn and make your foraging trips more exciting.

As the sun began to set, the Wilderness Explorers returned to their campsite. They laid out their finds and enjoyed a meal straight from the forest. The dandelion salad was crisp and fresh, the clover added a unique flavor, and the berries were the perfect dessert. They had gathered their dinner and learned valuable lessons about nature and survival. The forest had provided them with more than just food; it had given them knowledge, confidence, and unforgettable memories.

5.2 Safe Plants to Eat and How to Identify Them

Imagine being out in the wild and feeling like a botanist on a mission. Your goal? To identify safe plants you can munch on without a tummy ache. But remember, proper identification is vital. Eating unidentified plants can be a risky business.

Some plants look delicious but can be toxic. Always have an adult with you when foraging, and use field guides or apps to ensure you're picking the right greens. It's like having a plant detective in your pocket, helping you make safe choices.

Dandelions are one of the easiest plants to identify and gather. They have bright yellow flowers and jagged leaves resembling lion's teeth. Every part of the dandelion is edible. The leaves can be tossed into a salad, the flowers can be fried into fritters, and the roots can be roasted. Clover is another safe bet. This three-leafed plant has small, white or pink flowers and is often found in meadows. The leaves can be eaten raw or added to salads for a fresh, slightly sweet flavor. Chickweed is another plant you might come across. It has small, star-shaped white flowers and tiny leaves that form a dense mat on the ground. Chickweed leaves are tender and can be eaten raw, making them perfect for a fresh, wild salad. Wild onions are a real treat. You can identify them by their long, slender leaves and the distinct onion smell. The entire plant, from the bulb to the leaves, is edible and adds a delicious, mild onion flavor to your dishes.

Plantain is a plant you might recognize from your backyard. It has broad, oval leaves with prominent veins and tiny, inconspicuous flowers. You can eat the leaves raw or cooked.

They have a slightly bitter taste when raw but become milder when cooked.

Wild mint is a real treat. Its aromatic leaves can be used in teas, salads, or chewed for a refreshing flavor. The key to identifying mint is its distinctive smell. Rub the leaves between your fingers and take a sniff. If it smells minty, you're good to go

To identify these plants accurately, you must look closely at their features. Chickweed has tiny, star-shaped white flowers and small, oval leaves that grow close to the ground. Wild onions have long, slender leaves and small white or purple flowers. The pungent onion smell is a dead giveaway. Pay attention to the habitat and growing conditions. Dandelions and clover thrive in sunny, open areas, while chickweed prefers shady, moist spots. Wild onions can be found in meadows and forest edges.

When foraging for wild plants, safety is crucial. Always harvest from clean, uncontaminated areas. Avoid busy road-sides and places that might be polluted. Wash the plants thoroughly before eating to remove any dirt or bugs. It's like preparing a feast straight from nature's kitchen.

Foraging is like a treasure hunt, but you find delicious and nutritious plants instead of gold. Just remember, proper identification is the key to a safe and enjoyable foraging adventure. Always have an adult with you, use reliable guides, and trust your senses. Happy foraging!

5.3 Edible Berries - Sweet Treats in the Wild

Imagine the joy of stumbling upon a hidden patch of wild berries during your adventure. The natural sweetness and burst of flavor make foraging for berries fun and incredibly rewarding. These juicy gems are nutritious, providing a healthy snack that tastes like nature's candy. But before popping berries into your mouth, you must learn to distinguish between edible and poisonous varieties. Being able to tell them apart is a crucial skill, ensuring your foraging experience is safe and enjoyable.

One of the most delightful finds in the wild is the blueberry. These small, round berries are a lovely shade of blue and have a sweet taste that makes them a favorite among young explorers. Blueberries grow on bushes that are often found in sunny spots. The leaves are small and elliptical, and the berries grow in clusters. Raspberries are another treat you might encounter. They can be red or black and are made up of tiny drupelets that give them a unique texture. Raspberry bushes have thorny stems, so be careful when picking them. The leaves are serrated, and the berries grow at the tips of the stems.

Blackberries are similar to raspberries but dark purple or black when ripe. They have a sweet and tart flavor that makes them perfect for snacking or making into jams. Blackberry bushes also have thorny stems, so watch your fingers. The leaves are large and have three to five leaflets. Strawberries are smaller, red, and heart-shaped, and they have a sweet taste that is hard to resist. Wild strawberries grow low to the ground, and their leaves are trifoliate, meaning they have three leaflets.

Accurate identification of these berries involves several steps:

1. Observe the berry's color, size, and shape.
   Blueberries are small and round, raspberries are red or black and composed of drupelets, blackberries are dark and shiny, and strawberries are small and heart-shaped.
2. Examine the plant's leaves and stems. Blueberry bushes have small, elliptical leaves; raspberry leaves are serrated; blackberry leaves are large with multiple leaflets; and strawberry leaves are trifoliate.
3. Taste a small sample of the berry, but only if you are sure it is safe and have an adult with you.

Foraging for berries requires some practical safety tips to ensure a positive experience.

First, avoid areas near roads or places that might have been treated with pesticides. These chemicals can contaminate the berries and make them unsafe to eat. Always ensure the berries you pick are fully ripe. Unripe berries can be sour or even harmful. Ripe berries are usually vibrant in color and easy to pick. Once you've gathered your berries, wash them thoroughly before eating. This removes any dirt, bugs, or residues that might be on the surface.

Foraging for berries is an adventure that combines the thrill of discovery with the joy of tasting nature's sweets. So, watch for these delicious treats next time you're out exploring. With the proper knowledge and a bit of practice, you'll be able to safely identify and enjoy the wild's bounty.

5.4 Plants to Avoid - Staying Safe

What if you're exploring the wilderness, feeling like a true adventurer, when you come across a plant with shiny, three-leaf clusters. It looks innocent enough, but this is where knowing which plants to avoid becomes crucial. Poisonous plants can turn a fun foraging trip into a nightmare if you're not careful. Consuming toxic plants can lead to serious health issues, and it's essential to recognize the symptoms of plant poisoning. These can include nausea, vomiting, dizziness, and rashes. If you suspect you've ingested something toxic, seek immediate help. Identifying dangerous plants is just as important as knowing which plants are safe to eat.

NIGHTSHADE   **HEMLOCK**

One of the most common poisonous plants you might encounter is poison ivy. Its three-leaf clusters can cause itchy rashes that are anything but fun. The old saying, "Leaves of three, let it be," is a helpful reminder to steer clear. Another plant to watch out for is the deadly Nightshade. This plant has small, purple flowers and shiny black berries that look tempting but are highly toxic. Hemlock is another dangerous plant. It has fern-like leaves and small white flowers, and it's incredibly toxic if ingested. Lastly, foxglove, with its tall stalks of bell-shaped flowers, is beautiful but deadly. Ingesting any part of this plant can be lethal.

Recognizing these plants involves paying close attention to their characteristics. Poison ivy's three-leaf arrangement is a key feature, with each leaf having a smooth or slightly toothed edge. Deadly Nightshade has oval leaves and small, star-shaped purple flowers. Its berries are shiny and black and grow in clusters. Hemlock's leaves are finely divided, resembling parsley or carrots, and it has small white flowers grouped in umbrella-like clusters. Foxglove stands out with its tall spikes of tubular flowers, which can be purple, pink, or white.

Safety precautions are a must when foraging. Wear long sleeves and gloves to protect your skin from accidental contact with toxic plants. If you come across a plant you're unsure about, avoid it. It's better to be safe than sorry. Always wash your hands and tools thoroughly after foraging to remove any potential toxins. This simple step can prevent accidental ingestion or skin irritation

Let's make this a bit more interactive with a safety checklist. Imagine you're preparing for a foraging trip. Before you head out, review this checklist to ensure you're ready to stay safe:

- Wear long sleeves and gloves
- Carry a field guide to identify plants
- Avoid unknown plants unless correctly identified
- Wash hands and tools thoroughly after foraging
- Be aware of common poisonous plants in your area

Staying safe while foraging is all about knowledge and preparation. By learning to identify poisonous plants and taking the proper precautions, you can enjoy your time in the wild without worry. So, arm yourself with this knowledge, and you'll be well on your way to becoming a confident and safe forager.

As we wrap up this chapter, remember that the wilderness contains delicious treats and hidden dangers. Knowing what to pick and avoid is vital to a successful foraging adventure. Now that you're equipped with the know-how, you're ready to explore further.

Building the Perfect Shelter

You're deep in the forest, the sky darkens, and the wind begins to howl like a pack of wolves. The temperature drops, and you feel a few raindrops on your face. You look around at your friends and realize—you need a shelter, and fast! This chapter will show you how to build the perfect shelter to keep you safe and dry.

6.1 The Explorers Build Shelter in a Storm!!

Wilderness Explorers, Emily, Jack, Mia, and Sam, were on an epic quest for treasure. They had been hiking all day, their spirits high and their backpacks full of gear. As they trekked deeper into the forest, Emily noticed the sky turning a menacing shade of gray. "Guys, I think a storm is coming," she said, pointing to the dark clouds gathering above them.

The wind picked up, rustling the leaves and making the trees sway. Jack felt a chill run down his spine. "We need to find shelter, and fast," he said, looking around for a suitable spot. The group quickly huddled together, weighing their options. They needed a shelter that was quick to build and sturdy enough to withstand the storm.

Mia, ever the leader, suggested, "Let's build a lean-to shelter. It's simple and effective, and we can use the materials around us." The team sprang into action, gathering long, sturdy branches for the main structure and smaller twigs for support. They worked quickly, knowing they had to beat the approaching storm.

As they gathered materials, the first raindrops began to fall. The ground became slippery, and the branches were wet and heavy. "This is tougher than I thought," Sam muttered, struggling to carry a heavy branch. But the team didn't give up. They used their team-work and determination to overcome the challenges. Emily found some dry leaves under a fallen log, perfect for insulation. Jack used his multi-tool to cut and trim the branches, making them easier to handle.

With the main structure in place, they secured the branches with rope, tying them tightly to withstand the wind. Mia used a tarp they had packed to cover the shelter, creating a waterproof roof. They reinforced the sides with extra branches and leaves, ensuring the shelter was stable and secure. The wind howled, and the rain poured down, but inside their lean-to, the explorers were safe and dry.

They huddled together, feeling a sense of accomplishment. They had built a sturdy shelter in record time, using nothing but their wits and the materials around them. The storm raged outside, but they were warm and protected inside their lean-to. "We did it!" Emily exclaimed, her face beaming with pride.

As they waited out the storm, they talked about the lessons they had learned. Acting quickly and efficiently was crucial. The storm had come on fast, and they had to work as a team to build the shelter in time. Each member of the group had played a vital role. Emily's keen eye for materials, Jack's problem-solving skills, Mia's leadership, and Sam's strength all contributed to their success.

The experience taught them the importance of being prepared and working together. In the wilderness, challenges can arise at any moment, and knowing how to respond is key. The explorers had learned that they could overcome any obstacle with teamwork and determination. As the storm passed and the sky cleared, they emerged from their shelter, ready to continue their adventure.

Interactive Exercise: Build Your Own Lean-To Shelter

Why not try building your own lean-to shelter? Grab some friends and head to a safe, wooded area. Gather long branches for the main structure and smaller twigs for support. Use rope or cord to secure the branches, and cover the shelter with a tarp or leafy branches. Test its stability by gently pushing on the structure. Remember, teamwork and creativity are essential. Have fun, stay safe, and see if you can create a shelter as sturdy as our Wilderness Explorers!

6.2 Shelter Essentials: Why Shelter is Important

Imagine being out in the wild, and suddenly, the weather turns. Rain starts pouring down, and the wind picks up speed. A shelter isn't just a cozy hideaway; it's your shield against nature's whims. Staying dry is crucial. Wet clothes can sap your body heat, making you shiver uncontrollably. This can lead to hypothermia, a dangerous drop in body temperature in cold weather. On the flip side, in hot climates, a shelter provides shade, protecting you from the sun's relentless rays and helping you avoid heat exhaustion. It's like having an invisible force field that keeps the elements at bay.

Choosing the right location for your shelter is like picking the perfect spot for your secret base. You would want to avoid setting up in a low-lying area that might flood if it rains. Instead, look for higher ground where water won't pool. Natural windbreaks like trees or rocks are your allies, shielding you from gusts that can turn your shelter into a kite.

Ensure the ground is flat and free of sharp objects that could poke through your sleeping bag or tarp. No one's idea of a good night's sleep is a lumpy, rocky bed. Think of it as scouting the best campsite in a crowded campground—only you get first dibs!

Building a sturdy shelter involves a few basic principles. Stability is key. You don't want your shelter collapsing in the middle of the night. Use strong branches and secure them well. Insulation is another crucial element. Your shelter should keep warmth inside and the cold outside. Layers of leaves, grass, or even your clothes can provide insulation. Ventilation is equally important. Condensation can build up without proper airflow, making everything damp and musty. A well-ventilated shelter, like a breathable yet cozy tent, ensures you stay dry and comfortable.

When it comes to materials, nature offers a treasure trove. Branches and sticks form the backbone of your shelter, providing structure and support. Look for long, sturdy branches for the main frame and smaller sticks for cross-support. Leaves and grass are excellent for insulation. They trap heat and keep the cold at bay. Rocks and logs add stability, anchoring your shelter to the ground. They're like the pegs and poles of a tent, only more rugged and natural. Use what you find around you, and don't hesitate to get creative.

6.3 Lean-To Shelters – Simple and Effective

You'll need a shelter, and you need it fast. A lean-to shelter is your best bet. It's a simple structure with one wall and a sloping roof, making it quick and easy to build. This type of shelter is perfect for mild weather conditions and requires minimal materials. It's like nature's version of a quick fix, but way cooler.

To build a lean-to shelter, you'll need some basic materials. First, gather long, sturdy branches or poles. These will form the main structure of your shelter. You'll also need smaller sticks and twigs for cross-support. You can use leafy branches or a tarp if you have one for the roof. Finally, rope or cord is essential for securing the structure. Think of these materials as your building blocks, and you're the architect of your little woodland house.

Start by finding a suitable location. Look for a natural support, like a tree or a large rock, where you can anchor one end of your shelter. Place the long branches at an angle, leaning them against the tree or rock to form the main framework. Make sure the branches are secure and won't slip. Use the smaller sticks and twigs to create cross-support, weaving them between the long branches. This will add stability to your shelter. Secure everything tightly with rope or cord. Now, it's time to add the roofing materials. Lay leafy branches or a tarp over the framework, ensuring they overlap to create a weatherproof cover. Your lean-to shelter is now ready to protect you from the elements.

Making your shelter comfortable and safe is just as important as building it. To insulate your shelter, use leaves or grass as bedding. This will keep you warm and add a bit of cushioning.

Test the stability of your structure by gently pushing on it. If it feels wobbly, reinforce it with more branches or rope. Keep the entrance of your shelter facing away from the wind to prevent drafts. This way, you'll stay cozy and protected inside.

Visualize you're out in the wild, and you've just finished building your lean-to shelter. You step back and admire your handiwork. The structure stands tall and sturdy, ready to shield you from the weather. You gather some leaves and grass, spreading them out inside the shelter to create a soft, insulating bed. As you crawl inside, you feel a sense of accomplishment. You've built a safe haven with your own hands, using the materials around you and your survival skills. The wind howls outside, but you're warm and secure inside your lean-to.

Building a lean-to shelter is not only practical but also a rewarding experience. It's a chance to connect with nature and test your survival skills. You can create a sturdy, weatherproof shelter with a few simple materials and effort. So, next time you find yourself in the wild with dark clouds looming overhead, remember the lean-to shelter. It's your quick and effective solution to staying safe and dry.

6.4 Debris Huts for Cold Weather

The cold wind is biting at your cheeks and the snow crunching beneath your boots. It would help if you had a shelter that would keep you warm through the night. Enter the debris hut: a compact structure that traps body heat, perfect for cold weather. Think of it as nature's version of a cozy sleeping bag, using materials you can find lying around. The beauty of a debris hut is that it uses what's readily available in the wild—leaves, grass, and branches—to create an insulated haven that guards against the cold.

To build a debris hut, you'll need a few essential materials. Start with a large, sturdy branch or pole for the ridgepole. This will act as the backbone of your shelter. You'll also need smaller branches for the ribbing structure, which supports the insulating layers. Gather large amounts of leaves, grass, and other debris for insulation. The more, the better. These materials will trap your body heat and keep the cold out. You don't need fancy tools; just your hands and some creativity.

First, find a suitable location for your debris hut. Look for a natural windbreak, like a cluster of trees or large rocks, to shield your shelter from the wind. You'll want to place the ridgepole between two supports, such as logs or rocks, to form the main structure. The ridgepole should be long enough to accommodate your body, with extra room for comfort. Once the ridgepole is secure, start creating the ribbing structure with smaller branches. Arrange them at an angle along the ridgepole, forming a frame resembling a tent's skeleton.

Next, it's time to pile on the debris. Cover the entire structure with leaves, grass, and any other insulating materials you can find. The goal is to create a thick layer that will trap heat and keep the cold out. Don't be shy—pile it on until your shelter resembles a giant mound of leaves. The more insulation, the warmer you'll be. Make sure to leave a small entrance at one end, just big enough to crawl through.

To make your debris hut more comfortable and safe, consider creating a small entrance to minimize heat loss. You can use additional debris to create a door or flap that you can close once you're inside. This will help keep the warmth in and the cold air out. Spend a short time inside your hut to test the insulation. If it feels too cold, add more debris until it's snug and warm. Remember, the goal is to create a cozy, insulated space to keep you comfortable through the night.

Picture yourself crawling into your debris hut as the sun sets and the temperature drops. The walls of leaves and grass surround you, creating a warm, insulated cocoon. You close the entrance flap, sealing in the warmth. As you lie there, you feel the cold wind outside, but it's cozy and comfortable inside your hut. You've built a shelter that keeps you warm and gives you a sense of accomplishment. You've used your skills and the materials around you to create a safe haven in the wilderness.

6.5 Tarp Shelters – Quick and Easy

Picture this: You're out exploring the wild, and suddenly, the sky turns gray, and you know a downpour is coming. Enter the tarp shelter, your versatile, go-to solution for quick and easy protection. A tarp is lightweight and easy to carry, making it an ideal choice for any adventure. It's quick to set up and take down, and you can adapt it to various environments and weather conditions. Think of it as your portable fortress, ready to deploy whenever and wherever you need it.

To build a tarp shelter, you'll need a few basic materials. First, you need a durable tarp or a large plastic sheet. This is the main cover, shielding you from rain, wind, and even the sun. Next, grab some rope or cord to secure the tarp. Tent stakes or sturdy sticks are also essential for anchoring the corners. These materials are easy to pack and carry, making them perfect for any young explorer.

Setting up a tarp shelter is like playing with a giant piece of origami. You can create several types, depending on your needs and the environment. The basic A-frame shelter is a classic. Find two trees standing a few feet apart. Secure the tarp between them, forming a ridge line. Stake down the sides to create a tent-like structure. It's simple, effective, and gives you plenty of space inside.

For a lean-to shelter, anchor one side of the tarp to the ground using stakes or heavy rocks. Pull the other side up and secure it to a tree or pole, creating a slanted roof. This design is perfect for blocking wind and rain from one direction. If you're looking for more coverage, try a diamond fly shelter. Lay the tarp flat and stake down one corner. Lift the opposite corner and secure it to a tree or pole, creating a diamond-shaped canopy. This setup provides excellent protection from the elements while giving you more headroom.

Maximizing the effectiveness of your tarp shelter involves a few essential techniques. First, ensure the tarp is tightly secured to prevent flapping. Loose tarps can make a racket in the wind and might even blow away. Use extra rope or cord to tie down any loose edges. Creating a drip line can also help divert rainwater away from your shelter. Run a small rope from the tarp to a spot on the ground, allowing water to follow the rope instead of dripping inside. Lastly, natural surroundings should be used to enhance stability and protection. Anchor your tarp to rocks, trees, or fallen logs to keep it secure and steady.

Building a tarp shelter is not just about staying dry; it's about using your creativity and resourcefulness to adapt to any situation. Whether you're facing a sudden rainstorm or need shade on a hot day, a tarp shelter is your versatile go-to solution. So, next time you're out exploring, and the weather takes a turn, grab your tarp and transform your surroundings into a cozy, protected haven. And remember, every great explorer knows that the key to survival is being prepared for anything.

7

Weather Awareness

You're out in the wild, the sun shining brightly as you hike through the forest with your friends. Birds are singing, and everything seems perfect. Suddenly, you notice the sky darkening, and the wind starts to pick up. The air feels different, and you sense a storm might be coming. This is where your weather awareness skills become crucial. Understanding the signs of changing weather can help you stay safe and make the most of your adventure.

7.1 The Explorers Predict the Weather!!

Emily, Jack, Mia, and Sam—find themselves in this situation. On a sunny morning, they decide to hike deeper into the forest, excited about the day's adventure. As they walk, Emily notices the shape of the clouds changing. They're no longer fluffy and white but starting to look dark and heavy. "Guys," she says, pointing to the sky, "I think the weather is about to change."

Jack, always the gadget enthusiast, pulls out his small weather guide. "These clouds look like nimbus clouds," he says. "They're often a sign that heavy rain or a thunderstorm is coming." The group stops and looks around, realizing they need to make a plan. The wind picks up, rustling the leaves and making the trees sway. Mia feels a sudden drop in temperature and knows they need to act fast.

Using everyone's skills, they determine their course of action. Emily suggests they head to a nearby clearing they passed earlier, which seemed like a good spot to set up a temporary shelter. Jack agrees, adding, "We need to find materials to build a shelter that keeps us warm and dry." Sam, ever the storyteller, makes a quick joke about building a fortress to keep out the storm dragons, lightening the mood and keeping everyone calm.

They quickly gather branches, leaves, and a tarp from their packs. The safety expert, Mia reminds everyone to stay close and work together. They decide on a lean-to shelter, as it's quick to build and effective. Emily and Jack start by securing long branches against a sturdy tree, creating the main framework. Sam and Mia gather smaller sticks and leaves, adding them to the structure for insulation. They use the tarp to cover the roof, ensuring it's tightly secured to keep out the rain.

As they work, the sky grows darker, and the first raindrops begin to fall. The explorers hurry to finish their shelter, securing the last branches and ensuring everything is in place. The rain starts pouring down as they complete their task, and the wind howls around them. They huddle inside their lean-to, feeling a sense of accomplishment.

Interactive Exercise: Weather Prediction Journal

Why not start your own weather prediction journal? Grab a notebook and record the weather each day. Note the types of clouds you see, the wind direction, and any temperature changes. Over time, you'll notice patterns and improve your weather prediction skills.

The storm rages outside, but the explorers are warm and dry inside their shelter. They share stories and snacks, feeling proud of their teamwork and quick thinking. As the storm passes and the sky clears, they leave, ready to continue their adventure. Their weather awareness skills have kept them safe and made their journey even more exciting.

7.2 Reading the Clouds - Predicting Weather

Envision looking up at the sky and seeing a canvas painted with different types of clouds. Each cloud tells a story about the weather, and knowing how to read them can help you plan your day in the wild. Let's start with cirrus clouds. These thin, wispy clouds look like delicate feathers high up in the sky. They often indicate fair weather, so you can usually expect a nice day if you see them. Then there are cumulus clouds, those big, fluffy ones that look like cotton balls. They typically mean good weather, too, but keep an eye on them—they can develop into thunderstorms if they start towering and darkening.

Now, let's talk about stratus clouds. These are low-lying and gray, spreading out like a thick blanket across the sky. They often bring drizzle or light rain, so if you see stratus clouds, it's a good idea to have your rain gear handy. Lastly, we have nimbus clouds. These dark and dense clouds are the real troublemakers, usually associated with heavy rain or storms. If the sky fills with nimbus clouds, it's time to find shelter and prepare for a downpour.

To predict weather changes, start by noting the height and thickness of the clouds. High, thin clouds often mean stable weather, while low, thick clouds can indicate incoming precipitation. Pay attention to how fast the clouds are moving and in which direction. Fast-moving clouds can signal changing weather, especially if they're coming from the west. Also, watch for changes in cloud color and shape. A darkening sky often means a storm is brewing.

Practical Cloud Watching Activity

Create a cloud observation journal. Grab a notebook and spend some time each day looking at the sky. Draw and label the different cloud types you see, noting their height, shape, and movement. Make daily weather predictions based on your observations and see how accurate you can be. This activity will sharpen your weather prediction skills and make you feel like a true meteorologist.

Understanding cloud patterns is just one part of predicting the weather. Observing animal behavior can also provide valuable clues. Birds flying low often indicate an approaching storm, as they seek shelter. Insects becoming more active can signal rain, as they prepare for the moisture. Even changes in smell and sound can give you hints.

The scent of rain in the air or the distant sound of thunder can alert you to upcoming weather changes. The rustling of leaves in the wind might indicate an incoming front.

Using these observations can help you better plan your outdoor activities. For example, if you see cumulus clouds building up, you might finish your hike early to avoid a potential storm. If you notice stratus clouds rolling in, you might set up your camp with extra waterproofing. Cloud reading has limitations, though, and it's wise to use it alongside other weather prediction methods, like checking a weather app or listening to a weather forecast before heading out.

Reading the clouds and observing nature's cues can make your wilderness adventures safer and more enjoyable. So, next time you're out exploring, look up at the sky and see what the clouds are telling you.

7.3 Preparing for Rain - Staying Dry

Imagine you're trekking through the woods, and suddenly, the sky opens up, drenching everything in sight. Staying dry isn't just about comfort; it's crucial for your safety. Wet clothes can lead to hypothermia, even in mild temperatures. When your clothes get soaked, they lose their insulating properties, making it hard for your body to stay warm. Plus, nobody likes squishy socks and chattering teeth. Keeping your gear and supplies dry is equally important. A wet sleeping bag or soggy matches can turn a fun adventure into a miserable experience.

Choosing the proper rain gear can make a huge difference. Start with a waterproof jacket and pants. Look for materials like Gore-Tex or nylon with a waterproof coating. These materials are lightweight, breathable, and designed to keep you dry. Ensure the jacket has a hood to keep your head dry and adjustable cuffs to prevent water from seeping in. Waterproof boots and socks are a must. There's nothing worse than sloshing around in wet shoes. Look for boots made from rubber or treated leather, and pair them with moisture-wicking socks to keep your feet warm and dry.

Ponchos and rain covers are versatile options. A poncho can cover both you and your backpack, providing extra protection. They're lightweight, easy to pack, and can double as a ground cover or makeshift shelter. Rain covers for your backpack are also a good idea. They keep your gear dry and prevent water from seeping in through zippers and seams. When setting up camp, choose a location with natural windbreaks like trees or rocks. This will help shield you from driving rain and stabilize your shelter.

Practical tips for staying dry include packing extra dry clothing in waterproof bags. Sealable plastic bags or dry sacks work well. Keep a change of clothes in your backpack so you can switch to something dry if you get soaked. When hiking, avoid low-lying areas that might flood, and steer clear of open fields where you're more exposed to the elements. If caught in a downpour, look for natural shelters like overhanging rocks or dense tree cover. These can provide temporary relief until you can set up your own shelter.

Preparing for rain is about more than just staying dry; it's about staying safe and comfortable. With the right gear and a few practical tips, you can turn a rainy day into another exciting part of your adventure.

7.4 Keeping Warm in Cold Weather

Imagine you're on a winter hike, the air crisp and the ground covered in a light blanket of snow. As the temperature drops, staying warm becomes your top priority. The secret to staying cozy is layering your clothing, which works like a charm to trap heat and keep the cold at bay. Think of it as building your own personal fort against the chill.

Start with a base layer. This is the first layer that sits closest to your skin; its job is to wick moisture away. You don't want sweat clinging to you and making you cold.

Materials like polyester or merino wool are perfect for this. They pull the moisture away from your body, keeping you dry and warm. Think about wearing a snug-fitting long-sleeve shirt and leggings made of these materials—you're already off to a great start.

Next comes the insulating layer. This is where the real warmth happens. Think of it as the fluffy blanket that traps heat. Fleece jackets, down vests, or wool sweaters are excellent choices. They help retain your body heat, creating a cozy cocoon around you.

The outer layer is your shield against the elements. This layer protects you from wind, rain, and snow. A good outer layer should be both windproof and waterproof. Jackets made of materials like Gore-Tex or other breathable waterproof fabrics are ideal. They keep the wind from cutting through your layers and prevent moisture from seeping in. This layer is your final defense, ensuring all the warmth stays inside.

When dressing in layers, remember that you can always add or remove layers to regulate your temperature. If you feel too warm, peel off the insulating layer. If the wind picks up, zip up your outer layer. It's like having a customizable thermostat that you control. This flexibility is key to staying comfortable and avoiding overheating or getting too cold.

Let's remember your extremities. Keeping your hands, feet, and head warm is just as important. Wear insulated gloves or mittens to protect your hands. Wool or synthetic socks will keep your feet toasty, and waterproof boots ensure they stay dry. A warm hat or beanie traps heat that would otherwise escape from your head.

Try layering up for a day outside in different weather conditions to practice this. Note how each layer feels and how easy it is to adjust your temperature by adding or removing layers. This hands-on experience will help you understand the importance of each layer and how they work together to keep you warm.

Staying warm in cold weather is all about smart layering. Base layers wick away moisture, insulating layers trap heat, and outer layers protect you from the elements. You can turn a chilly day into a comfortable adventure with the right combination.

7.5 Protecting Yourself from the Sun

Stepping out into a sunny meadow, the sky a perfect blue with the Sun beaming down. While the warmth feels great, protecting your skin from the Sun's harsh rays is important. Wearing the correct clothing can make all the difference.

Start with long-sleeved shirts and pants. They might not sound like the coolest option, but they shield your skin from harmful UV rays. Choose light-colored, breathable fabrics like cotton or moisture-wicking materials to stay comfortable. A wide-brimmed hat is also a must. It provides shade for your face, neck, and ears, which are often the most exposed. Think of it as your portable shade tree. And remember sunglasses with UV protection. They'll keep your eyes safe and make you look cool while you're at it.

Sunscreen is another superhero in your sun protection arsenal. Look for a sunscreen with an SPF (Sun Protection Factor) of 30 or higher. The higher the SPF, the better it will protect you from the Sun's harmful rays. Apply it generously to all exposed skin, including your face, neck, and the backs of your hands. Remember those easy-to-miss spots like the tops of your ears and the back of your neck. Reapply every two hours, or more often if you're swimming or sweating. Sunscreen is like an invisible shield but needs regular recharging to stay effective.

Creating shade is another great way to protect yourself from the Sun. If you plan to stay in one spot for a while, set up a tarp or use natural covers like trees. A simple sun shelter can be made with a tarp, some rope, and a few sturdy sticks. Find a couple of trees to tie the rope between, drape the tarp over, and secure the corners with sticks or rocks. Instant shade! This keeps you cool and gives you a nice spot to relax and take a break from the Sun.

Staying hydrated is super important when you're out in the heat. Drink plenty of water throughout the day, even if you don't feel thirsty. Dehydration can sneak up on you and make you feel dizzy or tired or even give you a headache. Recognize the signs of dehydration: dry mouth, dark yellow pee, dizziness, and a lack of energy. If you notice any of these symptoms, take a break in the shade and drink some water. Carry a reusable water bottle and make it a habit to take sips regularly. You can also eat water-rich fruits like watermelon or oranges to help stay hydrated and get a tasty treat at the same time.

So, next time you're out enjoying a sunny adventure, remember to gear up with long sleeves, a wide-brimmed hat, and UV-protective sunglasses. Slather on that sunscreen,

create some shade, and keep yourself hydrated. Your skin and body will thank you, and you'll be ready to take on whatever the wild throws your way.

7.6 Safe Practices During Thunderstorms

Imagine you're out exploring, the sky suddenly turns dark, the wind picks up, and you hear a distant rumble. A thunderstorm is brewing. Understanding what causes these dramatic weather events is key to staying safe. Thunderstorms form when warm, moist air rises and cools, creating towering clouds. Inside these clouds, tiny ice crystals collide, generating static electricity. When the electrical charge builds up enough, it releases as a flash of lightning, followed by the booming sound of thunder. Lightning can strike trees, poles, and even the ground, making it very dangerous. Strong winds can also knock down branches, creating additional hazards.

Recognizing the signs of an approaching storm can give you a head start in finding safety. Watch for sudden changes in wind speed and direction—these can indicate that a storm is nearby. Notice if the sky darkens quickly or if clouds begin to race. Hearing distant thunder is a clear signal that a storm is coming. The saying "When thunder roars, go indoors" is a good rule. These signs help you prepare and find shelter before the storm hits.

When a thunderstorm is approaching, the first thing you should do is seek shelter. Find a safe, enclosed space like a building or a car. If you're in the wilderness and can't find a building, avoid tall objects like trees and poles, which are more likely to be struck by lightning. Stay away from water sources like rivers, lakes, and puddles, as water conducts electricity. If you're caught in the open with no shelter, crouch low to the ground with your feet together. This minimizes your risk of being struck by lightning. Avoid lying flat, as it increases your contact with the ground.

Preparing for thunderstorms, understanding the weather and being prepared are key skills for any wilderness explorer. Whether predicting a storm, staying dry in the rain, or keeping warm in the cold, these skills will help you make the most of your outdoor adventures. Let's look at some essential first aid skills in the next chapter to ensure you're ready for anything nature throws your way.

Essential First Aid

Walking through the forest with your friends suddenly, you hear a faint cry for help. Your heart races as you follow the sound, weaving through the trees until you stumble upon a hiker sitting on the ground, clutching their ankle in pain. This is where your first aid knowledge becomes invaluable. You're about to become a hero!

8.1 The Explorers Use Their First Aid Knowledge!!

Emily, Jack, Mia, and Sam were on one of their epic adventures when they heard the cry. It was faint but unmistakable. The team exchanged worried glances and quickly decided to investigate. They moved swiftly but carefully, navigating through the underbrush until they found a middle-aged hiker sitting on the ground, grimacing in pain. His ankle was swollen, and he looked visibly distressed.

Emily, always the first to jump into action, knelt beside the hiker. "Are you okay?" she asked, her voice calm and reassuring. The hiker, whose name was Mr. Thompson, explained that he had twisted his ankle while hiking and couldn't walk. Emily nodded, signaling to Jack and Mia. "We need to assess the injury and provide some first aid," she said.

Jack opened his backpack, pulling out their well-stocked first aid kit. Mia began examining Mr. Thompson's ankle. "It looks like a sprain," she said, noting the swelling and bruising. "We need to stabilize it and reduce the swelling." Sam, ever the storyteller, kept Mr. Thompson distracted with a tale about a brave knight who overcame a similar injury on his quest.

Mia instructed Jack to gently remove Mr. Thompson's shoe and sock, revealing the full extent of the swelling. "We need to use the RICE method—Rest, Ice, Compression, and Elevation," she explained. Jack nodded, retrieving the kit's elastic bandage and cold pack. "We'll start with the cold pack to reduce the swelling," he said, activating it and carefully placing it on the injured ankle.

Emily and Sam worked together to find two sturdy sticks to use as a makeshift splint. They positioned the sticks on either side of Mr. Thompson's ankle and secured them with the elastic bandage, providing the necessary support. "This will keep your ankle stable until we can get you to a doctor," Emily said, her voice filled with confidence. As they worked, Mr. Thompson couldn't help but smile at the young explorers' expertise. "You kids are amazing," he said, wincing slightly as Mia adjusted the bandage. "I've never seen such a capable group of young adventurers."

With the ankle stabilized, the next challenge was helping Mr. Thompson get to a safer location. Jack and Sam fashioned a simple stretcher using a tarp and some sturdy branches. "We'll carry you to the trailhead, where we can call for help," Jack explained. The team worked together, carefully lifting Mr. Thompson onto the stretcher and beginning the trek back.

Along the way, they encountered a few obstacles—rocks, uneven terrain, and even a curious squirrel that seemed determined to join the adventure. But the Wilderness Explorers were unfazed. They navigated each challenge with determination and teamwork, ensuring Mr. Thompson's safety every step of the way.

As they reached the trailhead, they were met by a group of hikers who had heard about the situation. One of them had a cell phone and quickly called for help. Mr. Thompson expressed his gratitude, his face filled with relief. "I can't thank you enough," he said. "You kids saved the day."

The Wilderness Explorers beamed with pride. They had used their first aid knowledge to help someone in need, proving that even young adventurers could make a big difference. They felt a deep sense of accomplishment as they watched the rescue team arrive and take Mr. Thompson to safety. They had not only helped a stranger but also gained a new friend.

Interactive Activity: Practice the RICE Method

To ensure you're ready for any first aid situation, practice the RICE method at home. Find a friend or family member to be your "patient" and follow these steps:

- Rest: Have your patient sit or lie down comfortably.
- Ice: Use a cold pack or a bag of frozen peas wrapped in a cloth to reduce swelling.

- *Compression: Gently wrap an elastic bandage around the injured area.*
- *Elevation: Raise the injured limb above heart level to reduce swelling.*

This hands-on practice will help you feel confident and prepared like the Wilderness Explorers.

8.2 Assembling a Basic First Aid Kit

Let's imagine you're in the middle of an exciting adventure, and suddenly, someone trips and scrapes their knee. What do you do? A first aid kit is like carrying a mini doctor's office in your backpack. It gives you immediate access to medical supplies, allowing you to treat minor injuries on the spot. This can prevent infections and complications, ensuring minor scrapes don't become major problems. Just think about how handy it would be to have bandages and antiseptic wipes ready when needed.

A well-stocked first aid kit should include various essential items. First, you'll need adhesive bandages in different sizes. These are perfect for covering minor cuts and scrapes. Next, pack some sterile gauze pads and adhesive tape. Gauze pads are great for more extensive wounds, and the tape will keep them securely in place. Antiseptic wipes and ointments are also crucial. They help clean wounds and prevent infections. Remember tweezers and scissors. Tweezers can remove splinters or debris from a wound, and scissors help cut tape or gauze. Disposable gloves are another must-have. They protect both you and the injured person from germs.

Personalizing your first aid kit can make it even more effective. Think about your specific needs and activities. If you're prone to allergies, include any personal medications you might need. Adding a small flashlight and a whistle can be incredibly helpful. The flashlight will ensure you can see what you're doing, even in low light, and the whistle can signal for help if needed. Packing extra supplies like insect repellent and sunscreen is also a smart move. These can prevent bug bites and sunburns, keeping everyone comfortable and safe.

Maintaining your first aid kit is just as important as assembling it. Regularly check the expiration dates on medications and ointments. Using expired products can be ineffective or even harmful. Replenish any used or missing items. If you've used all the bandages, replace them before your next adventure. Keeping the kit organized and easily accessible is also crucial. You want to avoid rummaging through a messy bag when someone needs help. Use small compartments or bags to keep everything in its place.

Consider creating a checklist to ensure your first aid kit is always ready. This way, you can quickly see what's in the kit and what needs to be replaced. Here's a simple checklist to get you started:

- Adhesive bandages (various sizes)
- Sterile gauze pads
- Moleskin
- Adhesive tape
- Antiseptic wipes
- Antiseptic ointment

- Tweezers
- Scissors
- Disposable gloves
- Personal medications
- Small flashlight
- Whistle
- Insect repellent
- Sunscreen

Regularly use this checklist to keep your kit up-to-date. A well-maintained first aid kit ensures you're always prepared for any minor injuries that might happen on your adventures. It's like having a safety net you can rely on, giving you the confidence to explore and enjoy the wilderness without worry.

8.3 Treating Cuts and Scrapes

Out for a little hike when suddenly, you slip and scrape your knee. Ouch! Or you're reaching for that perfect hiking stick and getting a small cut from a sharp edge. These minor injuries are all too common in the wild. Cuts and scrapes might seem small, but treating them properly is crucial to prevent infection and ensure they heal quickly.

Understanding the different types of cuts and scrapes can help you respond appropriately. Minor cuts often come from sharp objects like sticks or rocks, leaving a clean slice on the skin. Scrapes, however, usually occur when you fall or brush against rough surfaces, leaving a raw, red mark that can sting and bleed.

When you find yourself with a cut or scrape, your first step is to clean it thoroughly to prevent infection. Your first aid kit is your best friend here, stocked with all the essentials for wound care. Antiseptic wipes or antiseptic solution are perfect for cleaning the wound gently but effectively. Sterile gauze pads and adhesive bandages are next on the list, helping to cover the wound and keep it clean. Antibiotic ointment is also a must-have, as it protects the wound from bacteria and speeds up healing. And don't forget scissors and tweezers, which can help remove any debris or trim bandages to the correct size.

Now, let's talk about how to treat those pesky cuts and scrapes step-by-step. First, wash your hands thoroughly to avoid spreading germs to the wound. This might seem obvious, but it's a crucial step. Next, use an antiseptic wipe or solution to clean the wound. Be gentle, as the area is likely to be tender. Once the wound is clean, apply a thin layer of antibiotic ointment. This will not only prevent infection but also keep the wound moist, promoting faster healing. Cover the wound with a sterile gauze pad or an adhesive bandage, depending on the size of the wound. Make sure the bandage is secure but not too tight, allowing the wound to breathe. Check the wound regularly and change the dressing as needed, especially if it gets wet or dirty.

To make these instructions stick, let's practice with a fun activity. Grab a doll or a stuffed animal and your first aid kit. Pretend the doll has a cut or scrape, and go through the treatment steps. Start by washing your hands, then clean the wound with an antiseptic wipe. Apply some antibiotic ointment, and carefully cover the "wound" with a bandage. This hands-on practice will help you remember the steps and feel more confident when treating real injuries.

8.4 Handling Sprains and Strains

One sunny morning while hiking up a rocky trail, feeling like a true adventurer, suddenly you step on an uneven rock. Your foot twists awkwardly, and you feel a sharp pain shoot up your ankle. You might have just experienced a sprain. Sprains are injuries to ligaments, the rugged bands connecting bones, often caused by twisting or falling. They can result in pain, swelling, bruising, and limited movement.

On the other hand, strains are injuries to muscles or tendons which connect muscles to bones. Strains often occur from overuse or sudden, awkward movements, like sprinting to catch up with friends. Recognizing the symptoms—pain, swelling, bruising, and difficulty moving the injured area—is crucial for knowing how to react.

Your first aid kit should have a few key items when treating sprains and strains. Elastic bandages are great for compression and support, helping reduce swelling and stabilize the injury. Cold packs, or ice packs, are essential for reducing pain and swelling. Pain relievers like ibuprofen can help manage discomfort, **but always ask an adult before taking any medication**. Splints or support braces can immobilize the injured area, preventing further damage. Having these items handy ensures you're prepared to handle these common outdoor injuries effectively.

Now, let's dive into treating sprains and strains step-by-step. The RICE method—Rest, Ice, Compression, Elevation—is your go-to strategy. First, rest the injured area by stopping any activity that might worsen the injury. Next, apply ice or a cold pack to the injured area for 15-20 minutes every 1-2 hours. This helps reduce swelling and numb the pain. Compression involves wrapping the injured area with an elastic bandage. Start wrapping below the injury and work your way up, keeping the bandage snug but not too tight. Elevating the injured limb above heart level helps reduce swelling by allowing fluids to drain away from the injury. Following these steps will help you manage the injury and promote healing.

It's fun to practice! Find a friend or family member and pretend they've sprained their ankle. Use an elastic bandage to wrap the "injury," applying compression for support. Grab a cold pack and demonstrate how to apply it to reduce swelling. Elevate the injured limb using a pillow or cushion. This hands-on practice will help you feel confident and prepared when treating real sprains or strains in the wild.

Handling sprains and strains might seem daunting, but you can manage these injuries effectively with the proper knowledge and tools. Remember, the RICE method is your best friend regarding sprains and strains. So, next time you're exploring the great outdoors, you'll be ready to handle any bumps, twists, or strains that come your way.

8.5 Dealing with Insect Bites and Stings

Let's pretend you're deep in the woods, the birds are chirping, and you're having the time of your life. Suddenly, you feel a sharp sting on your arm. You look down and see a bee buzzing away, leaving behind a painful, swollen area. Insect bites and stings are common nuisances in the wild, but knowing how to treat them can make all the difference in your adventure.

Let's break down some common insect bites and stings and their symptoms. Mosquito bites are probably the most familiar. They leave itchy, red bumps caused by mosquito saliva. These little pests feast on exposed skin, especially at dusk and dawn. Then there are bee and wasp stings, which are more dramatic. They cause a painful, swollen area with a visible stinger left behind by the bee. Wasps, unlike bees, can sting multiple times, making them particularly pesky.

Tick bites are another concern. Ticks latch onto your skin and can stay there for days if not removed. Their bites cause small, red bumps with the tick often still attached. These critters can carry diseases, so removing them promptly is crucial. Lastly, spider bites can vary in severity. While most are harmless, some can cause red, swollen areas with possible blistering. In rare cases, bites from spiders like the black widow or brown recluse can lead to more severe symptoms.

Your first aid kit should be well-equipped to handle these bites and stings. Antihistamine cream or hydrocortisone cream is your go-to for reducing itching and swelling. Tweezers are essential for removing stingers or ticks safely. Alcohol wipes are perfect for cleaning the bite or sting area and preventing infection. Ice packs help reduce swelling and numb the pain, providing much-needed relief.

Treating insect bites and stings involves a few simple steps. First, clean the bite or sting area with an alcohol wipe. This removes dirt and bacteria, reducing the risk of infection.

Next, an antihistamine or hydrocortisone cream should be applied to lessen itching and swelling. If a bee has stung you, use tweezers to carefully remove the stinger by scraping it out, being cautious not to squeeze it, which can release more venom. For tick bites, use tweezers to grasp the tick as close to the skin as possible and pull it out steadily. After removing the stinger or tick, apply a cold pack to the area to reduce pain and swelling.

A practical way to practice would be to grab a sponge or similar material and pretend it has a stinger or tick embedded in it. Use tweezers to carefully remove the stinger or tick, practicing your precision. Next, apply some cream and bandage the area, just like in a real situation. This hands-on practice will make you more confident dealing with insect bites and stings.

Think back to our Wilderness Explorers. Imagine Emily gets stung by a bee while picking wildflowers. Jack quickly grabs the first aid kit and uses tweezers to remove the stinger from Emily's arm. Mia cleans the area with an alcohol wipe and applies antihistamine cream to reduce the swelling. Sam, always the storyteller, distracts Emily with a funny tale to keep her mind off the pain. Within minutes, Emily feels better, and the team is ready to continue their adventure.

Insect bites and stings can be a real pain, but with the right knowledge and tools, you can handle them like a pro. Being prepared means you can focus on the fun of exploring the wilderness, knowing that you can tackle any little surprises that come your way. So, pack your first aid kit, practice your skills, and confidently prepare for more adventures.

Remember, first aid is just one part of being a great explorer. Keep learning, stay curious, and always be ready for the next challenge nature throws at you. Now that you have essential first-aid skills, you can move on to the next exciting chapter: understanding and respecting wildlife.

9

Animal Encounters

Let's say you are hiking through a dense forest, the morning sun turning the dewy leaves into a sparkling tapestry. You and your friends are on the lookout for animal tracks, eager to see what creatures might be sharing the trail with you. Suddenly, you spot some tracks on the ground! "Look at this!" you exclaim! The group gathers around to examine the tracks, the adventure taking an unexpected and thrilling turn.

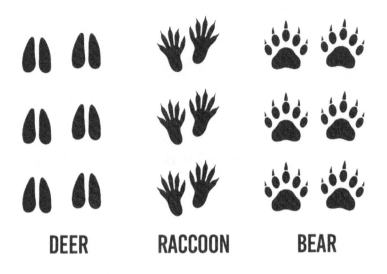

DEER   RACCOON   BEAR

9.1 The Explorers Find Animals!!

Emily kneels down, lightly running her fingers over the soft earth prints. "These look like deer tracks," she says, tracing the elongated shapes with her finger. Jack pulls out his field guide and confirms her guess. "Two elongated toes, definitely a deer," he agrees, grinning. The explorers follow the tracks, each step bringing them closer to a potential encounter with the majestic creature. They tiptoe, their eyes scanning the forest for any signs of movement.

As they continue, the tracks lead them to a small clearing. Suddenly, a rustling sound catches their attention. They freeze, their hearts pounding with excitement and a bit of nervousness. Mia whispers, "Stay calm and quiet." Slowly, a deer steps into view, its elegant form moving gracefully through the underbrush. The explorers watch in awe, careful not to make any sudden movements. The deer looks up, its ears twitching, before it bounds away, disappearing into the forest. The group lets out a collective breath, thrilled by the encounter.

Their adventure takes another turn when Sam spots something unusual on the trail. "Guys, look at this!" he calls out. The group huddles around to see a different set of tracks, smaller but distinct. "These must be raccoon tracks," Jack says, pointing out the five toes and the claw marks that resemble tiny human hands. The explorers follow the raccoon tracks, their curiosity leading them further into the woods. They imagine the raccoon's nocturnal adventures, scavenging for food and exploring its territory.

As they hike deeper into the forest, Emily suddenly stops, her eyes wide. "Bear tracks," she whispers, pointing to the large, unmistakable prints in the muddy ground. The group feels a mix of excitement and caution. Mia reminds everyone to stay calm and keep a safe distance. They continue on their path, talking softly to alert any nearby animals of their presence. The forest feels alive with unseen eyes watching their every move.

Their trek brings them to a sunlit rock, where they decide to rest and have a snack. Jack unwraps a granola bar when he spots something slithering nearby. "Snake!" he yelps, jumping back. The group quickly identifies it as a harmless garter snake, its slender body gliding gracefully over the rocks. They watch, fascinated, as the snake moves along, unbothered by their presence. Mia explains how to tell the difference between harmless and venomous snakes, pointing out the garter snake's distinctive stripes.

Interactive Exercise: Animal Track Journal

Create your own animal track journal! The next time you go on a hike, bring a small notebook and a pencil. Whenever you find tracks, draw them in your journal and note the location. Try to identify the animal using a field guide or an app. This way, you'll build a personal record of the animals you've encountered and learn more about their habits.

As the day winds down, the explorers continue their hike, feeling a deep connection with the wilderness and its inhabitants. Each track and rustle in the bushes tell a story, making their adventure more magical and memorable. They walk on, at peace with the forest and the creatures they share it with.

DEER   RACCOON   BEAR

9.2 Understanding Animal Behavior

It's like stepping into the animals' living room in the wilderness. They have their ways and habits; understanding these can make your adventure safer and more exciting. Animals behave in specific ways to survive, find food, and protect their territory. For example, many animals mark their territory using scents. This is their way of saying, "Hey, this is my space!" You might notice trees or rocks with scratch marks or a pungent smell. These are signs that an animal has claimed that area. It's like putting up a "Do Not Disturb" sign on your door.

During mating seasons, animals become more active and can behave differently. You might see birds performing elaborate dances or frogs croaking loudly at night. These activities are all about attracting a mate. It's like a wild dating game out there! Foraging and hunting patterns also play a big role in animal behavior. Animals are constantly looking for food, and you might see them during these times. Early morning and late afternoon are prime times for spotting animals on the move. They are searching for breakfast or dinner like you do at home.

Recognizing signs of aggression in animals is crucial for staying safe. If an animal feels threatened, it may try to warn you before it attacks. Growling, hissing, or making loud noises clearly indicates that an animal wants you to back off. Raised fur or feathers, stomping, or even a charging motion are other indicators that an animal is feeling aggressive. It's their way of saying, "Stay away!" If you notice any of these signs, it's best to slowly and calmly back away, giving the animal the space it needs to feel safe again.

Animals communicate using sounds, scents, and body language. Bird songs and calls can signal everything from warning about a predator to attracting a mate. Mammals often use scent markings to communicate. They might rub their scent on trees or rocks, leaving messages for other animals. Visual signals, like a tail flicking or ears twitching, are also common. These signals can convey a variety of messages, from friendliness to agitation. By paying attention to these clues, you can better understand what the animals are trying to say.

Respecting wildlife is essential when you're exploring their home. Always observe animals from a distance. Use binoculars to get a closer look without disturbing them. Avoid getting too close to nests or dens, as this can stress the animals and even provoke an attack. Remember, every creature is vital to the ecosystem, from the tiniest insect to the largest predator. By respecting their space and behavior, you help maintain the balance of nature.

9.3 Recognizing Animal Tracks

You're hiking along a trail and spot some curious marks in the dirt. Recognizing animal tracks is like reading a secret code left by nature's inhabitants. It can turn any walk in the woods into an exciting detective adventure. Understanding animal tracks helps you learn about behavior and habits and can alert you to potential risks or dangerous areas. For instance, coming across bear tracks might make you think twice about proceeding without caution. Plus, it's a fantastic way to learn about local wildlife and the ecosystem, making you feel like a true nature detective.

Let's talk about some familiar animal tracks you might encounter. Deer tracks are the easiest to spot. They look like delicate hoof prints with two elongated toes. These gentle creatures often leave their marks near water sources or open fields. Rabbit tracks are another common find. They have small, round front paws and elongated hind paws that almost look like tiny kangaroo prints. Raccoon tracks, on the other hand, resemble tiny human hands with five toes and claw marks. These curious critters are often found near streams or in wooded areas. Finally, fox tracks are oval-shaped, with four toes and a distinct triangular pad. Foxes are clever and elusive, so finding their tracks can be a thrilling discovery.

To identify and interpret animal tracks, you need to be observant. Start by looking at the tracks' size, shape, and pattern. Deer tracks, for example, are larger and more distinct compared to the smaller, rounder rabbit tracks. Next, note the distance between each track, known as the stride length. Longer strides often indicate a running animal, while shorter strides suggest a walking pace. Additional signs like scat, fur, or markings on trees can provide more clues about the animal's identity. For example, finding raccoon tracks near a tree with claw marks might indicate the raccoon climbed up recently.

Practical Tracking Activity

Why not set up a tracking trail in a safe area like your backyard or a local park? Use pre-made animal tracks or create your own using molds and soft clay. Scatter them along a path and invite your friends to follow the trail. Use field guides or apps to help identify the tracks and record your observations in a nature journal. This activity hones your tracking skills and makes for a fun and educational outdoor experience.

Recognizing animal tracks makes you more attuned to the world around you. Each track tells a story of the animal's journey through the wilderness, turning your hike into a captivating narrative of the wild. So, keep your eyes on the ground and your curiosity sharp—you never know what stories the tracks will reveal.

9.4 What to Do if You See a Bear

When you're out exploring the wild, you might come across one of the forest's most impressive residents: the bear. Understanding bear behavior can help you stay safe and appreciate these majestic creatures from a distance. You might encounter different types of bears, each with its unique traits. Despite their name, black bears can be black, brown, or even white. They are generally shy and avoidant of humans, preferring to scavenge for food like berries and insects. Grizzly bears, on the other hand, are larger and more aggressive. They have a distinctive hump on their shoulders and are known for being territorial. Understanding these differences is crucial because it helps you know what to expect and how to react.

When you're in bear country, safety precautions are your best friend. Making noise while hiking is a simple but effective way to avoid surprising a bear. Clap your hands, sing a song, or talk loudly with your friends. Bears have excellent hearing and usually steer clear if they know you're coming. Always keep a safe distance if you spot a bear. Never approach it, even if it seems calm. Bears can run much faster than you; you don't want to test that! Another essential tip is to store food and scented items securely. Bears have an incredible sense of smell and can be attracted from miles away. Use bear-proof containers or hang food bags from trees away from your campsite.

Let's talk about what to do if you actually encounter a bear. The first rule is to stay calm. Bears can sense fear, and panicking might make the situation worse. Slowly back away without turning your back on the bear. This shows the bear that you're not a threat. Speak in a calm, firm voice to avoid startling it. Say things like, "Hey bear, I'm just passing through." If the bear approaches you aggressively, it's time to use bear spray. Aim for the bear's face and spray in short bursts. Bear spray is highly effective and can stop a charging bear in its tracks.

Role-playing different bear encounter scenarios can be a fun and educational activity. Practice staying calm, backing away, and using the bear spray with a training canister. Learn to identify safe places to store food and scented items. This way, you'll be prepared and confident if you ever come face-to-face with a bear.

9.5 Safe Practices Around Snakes

Snakes are fascinating creatures that play a vital role in the ecosystem. You might encounter different types of snakes while exploring the wilderness. Non-venomous snakes, like common garden snakes, are harmless and beneficial. They help control pests by eating insects and small rodents. On the other hand, venomous snakes like rattlesnakes, copper-heads, and other dangerous species require more caution.

Understanding snake behavior is essential. Snakes are often misunderstood and feared, but they usually prefer to avoid humans. They might bask in the Sun to regulate their body temperature or hide under rocks to stay cool. Recognizing their behavior helps you appreciate their role in nature and keep them safe.

Identifying venomous snakes is crucial for safety, as they have distinctive markings and colors. For example, rattlesnakes have a rattle at the end of their tail that they shake as a warning. Copperheads have an hourglass pattern on their bodies. Observing head shape is another clue. Venomous snakes often have triangular heads, while non-venomous snakes have more rounded heads.

Additionally, recognizing their behavior can save you from danger. If a snake coils and rattles or hisses, it's giving a clear warning to stay away. Defensive postures like flattening their body or striking are signs that a snake feels threatened.

When you encounter a snake, staying safe is all about being aware and respectful. Stick to marked trails and avoid tall grass or rocky areas where snakes might hide. Always watch where you step and place your hands, especially when climbing or reaching into dark places. Never attempt to handle or provoke a snake, even if it appears harmless. If you encounter a snake, give it plenty of space to move away. Most snakes will not attack if they don't feel threatened.

If bitten by a snake, staying calm is your first line of defense. Panic can increase your heart rate, spreading venom faster. Keep the bitten limb immobilized and at or below heart level to slow the spread of venom. Call for emergency help immediately. Avoid traditional remedies like cutting the wound or sucking out venom, as these methods can cause more harm. Instead, focus on getting medical assistance as quickly as possible.

Practicing how to respond to snake encounters is a good idea. Use replicas or pictures in a controlled environment to identify different types of snakes. Practice staying still and calm if you see a snake, and learn how to safely move away. This way, you'll be prepared if you ever encounter a snake in the wild.

9.6 Protecting Your Food from Wildlife

Sharing your snacks with wildlife might sound fun when you're out in the wild, but it can lead to trouble. Bears, raccoons, and even squirrels can sniff out your food from miles away. Keeping your food safe from these curious critters is crucial. One way to do this is by using bear-proof containers. These containers are designed to withstand a bear's powerful claws and teeth, keeping your food secure. They might be bulky, but they can save you from a bear encounter. Hanging food bags from trees is another effective method. Find a sturdy branch at least 10 feet off the ground and hang your food bag using a rope. Make sure the bag is at least 4 feet away from the trunk to prevent animals from reaching it.

Setting up a separate cooking area away from your sleeping area is also essential. Designate a spot at least 100 feet from your tent for cooking and eating. This will help keep food smells away from where you sleep, reducing the chances of attracting wildlife to your campsite. After meals, clean up thoroughly. Leftover food scraps can attract animals, so make sure to wash dishes and utensils immediately. Dispose of any food waste properly by using designated trash bags and containers. If you have biodegradable waste, bury it away from the campsite to avoid attracting animals. For non-biodegradable trash, always pack it out with you. Leaving no trace ensures that the wilderness remains safe and clean for everyone.

Let's practice setting up a food storage system. Find a sturdy tree and practice hanging a food bag. Use a rope to hoist the bag up, making sure it's secure and out of reach. Role-play different scenarios where you might have to store food quickly, ensuring you're prepared for any situation. Proper food storage and waste disposal can make a big difference in keeping wildlife at bay and ensuring a safe and enjoyable camping experience.

9.7 Making Noise to Avoid Surprising Animals

The air is filled with rustling leaves and distant bird calls. But what if you suddenly stumble upon a wild animal? Making noise while exploring helps prevent surprising animals, avoiding potentially dangerous encounters. It's like giving wildlife a friendly heads-up that you're coming through, allowing them to move away and avoid an accidental confrontation.

There are several ways to make noise and alert animals to your presence. One of the easiest is simply talking or singing while you walk. You don't need to belt out a concert; just keeping a steady chatter with your friends can be enough to warn animals. Clapping your hands occasionally or using a whistle can also do the trick. Consider wearing bells on your backpack if you prefer a hands-free approach. The gentle jingling as you move creates a continuous sound that animals can hear from a distance, giving them plenty of time to clear the area.

Knowing when and how often to make noise is critical to its effectiveness. Make noise regularly along the trail, especially when entering a new area or if the vegetation is dense. Increase the noise levels in places with low visibility or where the terrain might hide animals. For example, if you're approaching a dense thicket or a bend in the trail, it's a good idea to clap your hands or call out to ensure any nearby animals know you're coming.

Interactive Activity: Noise-Making Practice

Let's practice making noise in different scenarios. Grab your friends and head to a wooded area. Start by walking through, talking or singing. Then, take turns using whistles and clapping at regular intervals. Finally, role-play encountering an animal by having one person pretend to be an animal while the others practice making noise to alert them. This activity will help you get comfortable with making noise and ensure you're ready to avoid surprising any wildlife on your adventures.

Making noise might feel silly at first, but it's an important skill for staying safe and respecting the wildlife you encounter. It turns your hike into a more interactive and engaging experience, allowing you to enjoy the beauty of nature without any unexpected surprises.

10

Specialized Skills for Different Environments

L et's pretend you are walking through a vast, golden desert, the sun blazing like a giant spotlight. The heat is intense, the air dry, and the landscape stretches endlessly in every direction. This isn't just any adventure—this is desert survival! The desert presents unique challenges, but with the right skills, you can navigate this harsh environment like a pro.

10.1 Desert Survival - Finding Shade and Water

Surviving in the desert is no walk in the park. The extreme heat can feel like you're inside an oven, and finding water is like searching for a needle in a haystack. Staying cool and hydrated is crucial. You need to be aware of the signs of heat exhaustion and dehydration. Heat exhaustion can make you feel dizzy, nauseous, and weak. Dehydration can cause dry mouth, dark yellow urine, and fatigue. If you start feeling any of these symptoms, it's time to take a break and drink some water.

Finding shade is your first line of defense against the scorching Sun. Look for natural features like rocks or shrubs that cast shadows. These can provide temporary relief from the heat. You can build your own if you can't find any natural shade. A simple shade shelter can be made using a tarp or blanket. Tie one end of the tarp to a couple of sturdy branches or rocks, and let the other end rest on the ground. This creates a sloping roof that will protect you from the Sun's direct rays. Another trick is to dig a shallow trench in the sand and lie in it during the hottest part of the day. The sand will be cooler than the surface, helping you stay comfortable.

Now, let's talk about water. In the desert, water is more precious than gold. Look for natural water sources like oases or dry riverbeds. Oases are rare but can be lifesavers, providing both water and shade. Dry riverbeds might still have moisture beneath the surface. Digging a small hole in the sand can sometimes reveal water. Another method to collect water is by using morning dew. Lay a cloth or plastic sheet overnight to catch the dew that forms early in the morning. Wring the cloth into a container to collect the precious droplets.

One of the most ingenious ways to get water in the desert is by using a solar still. This device uses the Sun's heat to extract water from the ground or vegetation. To make a solar still:

1. Dig a hole about a foot deep and place a container in the center.
2. Surround the container with green plants or wet sand.

3. Cover the hole with a clear plastic sheet, securing the edges with rocks or sand.

4. Place a small rock in the center of the sheet above the container, creating a dip. The Sun will cause the moisture to evaporate, condense on the plastic, and drip into the container.

It's like a magic trick for turning the desert's heat into life-saving water.

Conserving your energy and hydration is equally important. Move during the cooler parts of the day, like early morning or late evening. Avoid unnecessary physical exertion during the peak heat. Wear loose, light-colored clothing to reflect the Sun's rays and keep your body cool. When you drink water, take small, frequent sips rather than large gulps. This helps your body absorb the water more effectively and prevents wasting it.

Interactive Exercise: Desert Survival Simulation

Grab a notebook and pen. List the steps you would take if you were in a desert survival situation. Think about finding shade, locating water, and conserving your energy. Draw a simple diagram of a solar still and label its parts. Share your plan with a friend or family member and discuss how to improve it. This exercise will help you remember these critical survival skills and prepare you for any desert adventure.

Understanding the desert environment, staying cool and hydrated, finding shade, and locating water are key to surviving in this harsh landscape. With these skills, you can turn the desert into your personal playground, ready for any challenge it throws your way.

10.2 Forest Survival - Navigating Dense Woods

Visualize you are standing in a dense forest, the trees towering above you like ancient guardians. The canopy is so thick that sunlight barely reaches the forest floor, casting everything in a greenish twilight. The woods are full of life but can also be confusing and disorienting. The dense vegetation can make it hard to see landmarks, and losing your way is easy. Staying on marked trails is crucial. These paths are designed to guide you safely through the forest and prevent you from wandering into unknown territory. Straying off the trail can lead to getting lost, and in a place where every tree looks the same, that can be a real problem.

Natural landmarks are your best friends in the forest. Look for distinctive features like a huge rock, a tree with a unique shape, or a stream. These can help you keep track of where you are. Being aware of wildlife and potential hazards is also essential. The forest is home to many animals, some of which you might want to avoid meeting up close. Always stay alert and know what creatures inhabit the area you're exploring.

Navigating through dense woods requires a mix of old-school tools and natural signs. A compass and map are invaluable. Hold the compass flat in your hand, align the needle with the orienting arrow, and set your direction. Use the map to identify key landmarks and plot your course. But what if you don't have a map or compass? That's where trail markers come in handy. Break small branches or stack rocks to mark your path. This way, you can retrace your steps if needed. Follow natural landmarks like streams or ridgelines. Streams often lead to larger bodies of water or human settlements, and ridgelines can guide you through mountainous terrain. The Sun is another helpful guide. In the northern hemisphere, the Sun rises in the east and sets in the west. Use its position to maintain your direction.

The forest is a treasure trove of food if you know where to look. Edible plants and berries are plentiful, but you must know which ones are safe. Blueberries, blackberries, and raspberries are common in many forests and are easy to identify. Dandelions, clover, and plantain leaves are also edible and nutritious. Nuts and seeds are excellent sources of energy. Look for acorns, walnuts, and sunflower seeds. Fishing in streams and rivers can provide a steady food source. Use a simple fishing line and hook or make a small net. Setting traps for small game is another option, but only do this with adult supervision. Snares and deadfalls can be effective, but they require skill and practice.

The forest is a magical place full of secrets waiting to be discovered. But it also demands respect and preparation. Understanding the unique challenges of forest survival, from dense vegetation to potential hazards, can make your adventure safer and more enjoyable. Whether you're navigating with a compass, building a shelter from branches and leaves, or foraging for wild berries and nuts, these skills will help you thrive in the heart of the woods.

10.3 Coastal Survival - Resources by the Sea

Imagine standing on a sandy beach, the waves crashing rhythmically against the shore, the salty breeze tickling your face. Coastal environments offer unique challenges and resources that can make survival both exhilarating and tricky. Understanding tidal patterns is crucial. The tides change throughout the day, and knowing when the tide is high or low can help you avoid being stranded or swept away. Keep an eye on the waterline and remember that tides can rise quickly, covering areas that were exposed just a few hours earlier. Marine life is another important factor. While the ocean is teeming with creatures, not all are friendly or safe to eat. Recognize the difference between safe and dangerous marine life. For example, jellyfish stings can be painful and sometimes dangerous, so give them a wide berth. On the flip side, many types of seaweed are edible and nutritious, making them excellent resources for food. You can also find shellfish like clams and mussels, but always check for local advisories to ensure they are safe to eat.

Finding fresh water in coastal areas can be challenging since saltwater is abundant. One way to collect fresh water is by using tarps or containers to catch rainwater. Set up your tarp at an angle so the water flows into a container. You can also look for freshwater streams or springs that may flow into the ocean. These are often found near cliffs or rocky outcrops. If you can't find a natural source, you can use a solar still to desalinate seawater. Dig a hole in the sand, place a container in the center, and surround it with wet seaweed or vegetation. Cover the hole with clear plastic, securing the edges with rocks. Place a small rock in the center of the plastic to create a dip. The Sun will evaporate the water, condense on the plastic and drip into the container. It's like magic, turning saltwater into drinkable water.

Building a shelter on the coast involves using materials you find along the beach. Driftwood is a fantastic resource. You can construct a simple shelter by leaning large pieces of driftwood against each other to form a tent-like structure. Use smaller branches and seaweed to fill in the gaps and provide insulation. If you have a tarp, you can create a quick and effective shelter by anchoring it with rocks or sand. Lay the tarp over a sturdy framework of driftwood, and secure the edges with heavy objects to keep it from blowing away. Seaweed can also be used for insulation, providing an extra layer of warmth and protection from the elements.

Coastal areas are rich in food if you know where to look. Edible seaweed is plentiful and easy to identify. Look for types like nori, often found in sushi, or dulse, which is reddish and can be eaten raw or cooked. Fishing is another great way to find food. Use a simple fishing line and hook, or create a net from available materials. You can also gather crabs and other small marine creatures. Look for them under rocks or in shallow tide pools. Just be careful and avoid any creatures that look suspicious or unfamiliar.

While foraging, always be mindful of toxic marine life. Some shellfish can contain harmful toxins if ingested. Avoid shellfish that are closed tightly or have an off smell. Also, steer clear of brightly colored creatures, as they can often be venomous. When in doubt, it's better to leave it alone and look for safer options.

Interactive Exercise: Coastal Scavenger Hunt

Create a coastal scavenger hunt with a checklist of items to find, such as different types of seaweed, shells, driftwood, and safe marine life. This will help you practice identifying resources and better understand the coastal environment. Share your finds with friends or family and discuss their uses in survival.

Exploring the coastal environment is thrilling and rewarding. Whether you're collecting rainwater, building a driftwood shelter, or fishing for your dinner, the sea offers a wealth of resources that can make your coastal adventure unforgettable.

10.4 Mountain Survival - Staying Warm

You could be standing at the base of a towering mountain with crisp air and snow-covered peaks. The mountain environment presents unique challenges: cold temperatures, high altitudes, and rapidly changing weather. Staying warm and dry is crucial in these conditions. The cold can sneak up on you, and before you know it, hypothermia might set in. Hypothermia occurs when your body temperature drops too low. You might start shivering uncontrollably, feel confused, or even become sleepy. On the other hand, altitude sickness can make you feel dizzy, nauseous, headache and short of breath. Recognizing these signs early can help you take action and stay safe. Adaptability is key in the mountains, where the terrain is rugged and the weather can shift from sunny to stormy in minutes. If you know you will be hiking or climbing in higher altitudes that you are not accustomed to, plan on visiting the surrounding area for a few days before to acclimate, or ask your doctor for an anti-altitude sickness medication to take with you and follow its directions.

Finding and creating warmth is a top priority in the mountains. Building a fire is your first line of defense against the cold. Look for dry wood and pine needles, which catch fire quickly. Start small, with tinder and kindling, and gradually add larger logs. A reflective fire setup can maximize heat. Place a wall of rocks behind your fire to reflect the heat back towards you. This setup not only keeps you warm but also conserves fuel. Another clever trick is to use heated rocks. Place some stones near the fire, and once they're warm, wrap them in a cloth and place them in your sleeping area. These natural heaters can keep you cozy through the night.

Building a shelter in the mountains requires some ingenuity. A snow cave or trench can be an excellent choice, providing insulation from the cold. Dig into a snowbank to create a small cave, leaving a vent for air. The snow acts as an insulator, keeping the warmth and wind out. If there's no snow, a lean-to shelter is a great alternative. Find two sturdy trees and lay a long branch between them to form a ridge pole. Lean shorter branches against one side and cover them with leaves and smaller branches. This setup provides a windbreak and keeps you off the cold ground. If you have a tarp, use it to create a shelter with added warmth. Tie the tarp between two trees, and use rocks or stakes to anchor the corners. Adding windbreaks with branches or rocks can enhance the warmth and stability of your shelter.

Navigating the rugged terrain of mountains requires a keen eye and some planning. Always use a map and compass to stay on course. The landscape can be deceptive, with peaks and valleys that look similar. Natural landmarks like distinctive peaks, ridgelines, and valleys can guide you. Weather patterns in the mountains change rapidly. A clear day can turn into a stormy one within hours. Keep an eye on the sky and be prepared for sudden changes. Staying on marked trails is crucial. These paths are designed to guide you safely through the challenging terrain and prevent you from getting lost. Venturing off the trail can lead to dangerous situations, like getting trapped in unstable areas or losing your way.

Understanding the mountain environment and its challenges can turn a daunting experience into an exhilarating adventure. Stay aware of the signs of hypothermia and altitude sickness, and take action if you notice them. Finding and creating warmth is essential, whether by building a fire, using heated rocks, or constructing an insulated shelter. Navigating the rugged terrain with a map, compass, and natural landmarks ensures you stay on track. Staying on marked trails and being prepared for sudden weather changes can make your mountain adventure safe and enjoyable.

Mountains are majestic and awe-inspiring, offering breath-taking views and thrilling experiences. But they demand respect and preparation. With the skills to stay warm, navigate the terrain, and adapt to the ever-changing weather, you'll be ready to tackle any mountain challenge. So, gear up, stay warm, and embrace the adventure that awaits in the towering peaks and rugged valleys of the mountains.

11

Real-Life Scenarios and Practical Applications

L et's imagine that you're hiking with your friends on a beautiful day. The Sun is shining, birds are singing, and you're all having a great time exploring the forest. Suddenly, you realize that the trail looks unfamiliar. You glance around and notice that the trees and rocks all look the same. Your heart starts to race as it dawns on you—you might be lost. But don't worry! This chapter is your guide to handling real-life scenarios like this, turning a potentially scary situation into an adventure you can confidently navigate.

11.1 Lost in the Woods - What to Do?

First, staying calm is crucial when you realize you might be lost. Panic is your worst enemy in this situation. Take a few deep breaths to reduce the anxiety bubbling up inside you. Look around and note any landmarks or distinctive features that could help you later. Maybe there's a tree with a unique shape or a large rock formation. Listen carefully for any sounds indicating water, roads, or people. These sounds can guide you towards civilization.

Let's introduce the STOP method, a simple but effective way to handle the situation. STOP stands for Stop, Think, Observe, and Plan. First, stop moving. This prevents you from getting even more lost. Next, think about how you got to where you are. Try to remember any forks in the trail or landmarks you passed. Then, observe your surroundings. Look for useful resources like water sources, shelter materials, or signs of human activity. Finally, plan your next steps. Decide on the safest course of action based on your observations.

Creating a signal for help is one of the most important steps when you're lost. You want to make it as easy as possible for rescuers to find you. One effective method is arranging rocks or sticks to spell "SOS" in a clear, open area. Using bright clothing or materials to create a noticeable marker can also be very helpful. If you have the means and it's safe to do so, creating a smoky fire can attract attention from far away. Just make sure the fire is controlled and won't spread.

While waiting for help, staying put and safe is essential. Find a safe, open area where you can be easily spotted. Building a simple lean-to or debris shelter can provide protection from the elements. Use branches, leaves, and any other materials you can find to create a sturdy structure. Staying warm and dry is crucial, so use whatever you have—extra clothing, leaves, or even your backpack—to insulate yourself.

Interactive Exercise: Create Your Own SOS Signal

Grab some rocks, sticks, or other materials you can find and create a large "SOS" signal in your backyard or a nearby park. Make sure it's visible from above, just like it would be if you were lost in the woods. This exercise will help you understand the importance of making a clear, noticeable signal and give you practice in case you ever need to do it for real.

Staying calm, assessing your situation, and creating a signal are all critical steps in turning a potentially frightening experience into a manageable one. Remember, the wilderness can be challenging, but with the right skills and mindset, you can handle whatever comes your way.

11.2 Surviving a Night Alone – Staying Safe

You're out in the woods, and night is starting to fall. The shadows grow longer, the air gets cooler, and you realize you might have to spend the night alone. The first step to surviving a night in the wilderness is mentally and physically preparing for it. Accept the situation and focus on staying positive. This isn't the time to panic or feel defeated. Instead, take a deep breath and remind yourself that you have the skills and knowledge to overcome this. Conserve your energy by avoiding unnecessary movement. Instead of wandering around, stay put and keep your body calm. Staying hydrated and nourished with any available resources is crucial. Drink water if you have it, and munch on any snacks you might have packed. This will help keep your mind sharp and your body strong.

Building a night shelter is your next priority. Choose a safe location away from hazards like falling branches or animal trails. Look for a spot that's relatively flat and dry. Use natural materials to create insulation and weatherproofing. Gather sticks, leaves, and grass to build a sturdy frame. If you have a tarp or poncho, use it to create a roof. Make sure the shelter is stable and provides adequate protection from wind and rain. The goal is to create a cozy spot to stay warm and dry overnight.

Staying warm and comfortable is essential for a good night's rest. Use leaves, grass, or even extra clothing to insulate your shelter. Layer these materials to trap heat and keep the cold ground from sapping your warmth. If it's safe and you have the means, create a small fire for warmth. Just remember to keep it controlled and never leave it unattended. Staying dry is equally important. Ensure your shelter is well-built to keep out rain and wind. Use more leaves or grass to plug the gaps if you feel a draft.

Maintaining safety and vigilance is crucial as the night progresses. Keep a whistle and flashlight nearby. These tools can be lifesavers if you need to signal for help or illuminate your surroundings. Avoid risky movements or exploring in the dark. The wilderness can be unpredictable, and it's best to stay put once you've settled into your shelter. Stay alert for any signs of rescuers or help. If you hear voices or see flashlights, use your whistle or flashlight to attract attention. Staying vigilant ensures you take advantage of all opportunities for rescue.

As you settle into your shelter for the night, focus on staying calm and positive. Think of it as an adventure, a chance to test your skills and resilience. Listen to the sounds of the forest, feel the cool breeze, and watch the stars twinkle above. You might be alone, but you're not helpless. You can turn a night in the wilderness into a memorable experience with the right mindset and skills.

11.3 Creating Your Own Survival Plan

Let's say you're planning a big adventure. It could be a camping trip in the mountains or a weekend hike in the forest. You know it's going to be exciting, but what if things don't go as planned? That's where having a survival plan comes in. A survival plan is like your secret weapon for handling unexpected situations. It helps you stay prepared, reduces panic, and ensures everyone knows what to do in an emergency. Think of it as your adventure blueprint.

So, how do you create a survival plan? Start by identifying potential risks and hazards in the environment you'll be exploring. Are there wild animals in the area? Could the weather turn bad? Is there a risk of getting lost? Make a list of these potential dangers.

Next, think about the essential supplies and equipment you'll need. This includes water, food, a first aid kit, warm clothing, a flashlight, a map, and a compass. Write down everything you need to pack in your survival kit. Having a well-thought-out list ensures you remember everything important.

Another critical step is planning safe routes and meeting points for evacuation. Look at your map and mark the safest routes if you need to leave quickly. Identify safe spots where everyone can meet if you get separated. These could be landmarks like a big rock or a specific tree. Make sure everyone in your group knows these routes and meeting points. It's like having a secret code that everyone understands.

Practicing and testing your survival plan regularly is essential. Conduct practice drills with your family or friends. Pretend you're in a real emergency and follow your plan. This helps you see what works and what needs tweaking. You may find out that the route you chose is too difficult, or you may realize you need more water in your kit.

Reviewing and updating the plan based on feedback and experiences makes it more effective. Ensure everyone is familiar with the plan and their roles. This way, if an emergency does happen, everyone knows what to do without hesitation.

Keeping the plan accessible and updated is just as important as creating it. Store your survival plan in an easily accessible location, like a waterproof pouch in your backpack. Regularly review and update the plan as needed. You may find a new hiking trail or a change in the weather forecast, but keeping your plan current ensures it's always ready to use. Share the plan with trusted individuals and family members. This way, even if they're not with you, they know what to expect and can help if needed.

Having a survival plan is like having a superpower. It gives you the confidence to handle unexpected challenges and ensures you and your friends stay safe. So, the next time you're planning an adventure, take a moment to create your survival plan. It is the most important thing you pack.

Conclusion

As the Sun dipped below the horizon, casting a golden glow over the forest, our Wilderness Explorers—Emily, Jack, Mia, and Sam—sat around their campfire, reflecting on their adventures. They had navigated dense woods, built shelters in a storm, foraged for food, and even faced down a curious raccoon. They realized their success came from staying calm, working together, and being prepared. They had learned to trust each other and their skills, turning potential challenges into memorable experiences.

Emily looked at her friends and smiled. "You know what? We make a pretty great team," she said. Jack nodded, his eyes twinkling with excitement. "And we're ready for anything the wilderness throws at us!" Mia added, "We've learned so much. I can't wait to go on another adventure." Sam, always the storyteller, started weaving a new tale about their next journey, making everyone laugh.

They felt a sense of accomplishment as they packed up their gear and prepared to head home. They knew that this was just the beginning. The great outdoors was calling, and they were ready to

answer. They couldn't wait to plan their next adventure, knowing
that being outdoors was always the right thing to do.

Now, it's your turn. You've journeyed with Emily, Jack, Mia, and Sam through these pages, learning alongside them. You've discovered how to find water, build shelters, navigate the wild, and even handle unexpected encounters with wildlife. You've gained the skills and knowledge to face the wilderness with confidence. But remember, the adventure doesn't end here. It's just beginning.

Take what you've learned and apply it. Plan your own outdoor adventures with your family or friends. Create your own survival plans and practice your skills. Get out there and explore the world around you. The wilderness is a vast, beautiful, and exciting place, just waiting for you to discover its secrets. Whether you're hiking in the mountains, camping by a lake, or exploring a forest, the skills you've learned will help you stay safe, prepared, and confident.

Remember, every adventure is a chance to learn something new. Don't be afraid to make mistakes. They are part of the learning process. Embrace the challenges and celebrate your successes, no matter how small. Each time you step outside, you build your confidence and connection to nature.

As I, Brooks Wilding, have shared with you, the joy of the outdoors is truly special. It's a place where you can find peace, excitement, and a sense of freedom. There's nothing quite like the feeling of standing on a mountain peak, looking out over the world, or sitting by a campfire, surrounded by the sounds of the forest. These moments are what make life an adventure.

So, grab your gear, gather your friends, and head out on your next great adventure. The world is full of wonders, and it's all out there waiting for you. Be curious, be brave, and most importantly, have fun. The skills you've learned will guide you, and the memories you make will stay with you forever.

Ultimately, the true treasure isn't the destination but the journey itself. The laughter shared with friends, the challenges overcome, and the beauty of nature makes every adventure unforgettable. So, go out there and create your own stories. Let the wilderness be your playground, your classroom, and your inspiration. You've got this!

Here's to many more adventures filled with discovery, excitement, and the magic of the great outdoors. Always stay curious, keep exploring, and never stop learning. The world is your adventure, and it's up to you to make the most of it. Happy exploring!

References

- *Top 8 Outdoor Skills For Youth* https://koa.com/blog/top-outdoor-skills-for-youth/
- *Outdoor Safety for Kids • 7 Survival Tips for Any Scenario* https://www.osc.org/outdoor-survival-for-kids-7-safety-tips-for-any-scenario/
- *How To Make A Kid's Bug Out Bag - Mountain House* https://mountainhouse.com/blogs/emergency-prep-survival/how-to-make-a-kids-bug-out-bag#:
- *30+ Must-Read Fiction Books for Kids Who Love Nature ...* https://getthekidsoutside.com/fiction-nature-books-for-kids/
- *Bushcraft: How to Start a Fire with Flint and Steel* https://www.mensjournal.com/adventure/bushcraft-how-to-start-a-fire-with-flint-and-steel
- *Fire Safety for Children - U.S. Fire Administration* https://www.usfa.fema.gov/prevention/home-fires/at-risk-audiences/children/
- *8 Kid-Friendly Campfire Recipes For Your Next Family Camping Trip* https://www.lakelandtoday.ca/rv-lifestyle/8-kid-friendly-campfire-recipes-for-your-next-family-camping-trip-7229972
- *Magnifying Glass For Survival Fire Starting* https://modernsurvivalblog.com/survival-kit/a-magnifying-glass-for-survival/
- *Lean-to Shelters: How to Build a Lean-to Shelter in the Wild* https://www.masterclass.com/articles/lean-to-shelter
- *Debris Hut Construction* https://www.wildernesscollege.com/debris-hut.html
- *3 Ways to Build a Tarp Shelter* https://www.wikihow.com/Build-a-Tarp-Shelter
- *Outdoor Safety for Kids • 7 Survival Tips for Any*

Scenario https://www.osc.org/outdoor-survival-for-kids-7-safety-tips-for-any-scenario/

- *Finding water in the wilderness - Scouting magazine* https://scoutingmagazine.org/2019/04/finding-water-in-the-wilderness/
- *Water Treatment Options When Hiking, Camping or Traveling* https://www.cdc.gov/healthywater/drinking/travel/index
- *Best water purification tablets (and other portable purifiers)* https://theprepared.com/gear/reviews/portable-water-purification/
- *Making Water Safe in an Emergency* https://www.cdc.gov/healthywater/emergency/making-water-safe.html
- *How to Use a Compass and Read a Map - Little Passports* https://www.littlepassports.com/blog/educational/use-compass-with
- *Natural Navigation for Children* https://www.naturalnavigator.com/the-library/wildlife-watch/
- *30 Survival Skills Activities for Kids* https://www.educatorstechnology.com/2023/06/30-survival-skills-activities-for-kids.html
- *Creating and Using Trail Markers in the Wild - Texas Bushcraft* https://www.texasbushcraft.com/blogs/news/creating-and-using-trail-markers-in-the-wild#:~
- *A Beginners Guide to Foraging for Wild Edibles With Kids* https://wilderchild.com/blogs/news/foraging-for-wild-edibles-with-kids#:
- *10 Dangerous Plants and Fungi to Avoid While Foraging* https://outdoors.com/dangerous-plants-and-fungi-to-avoid-while-foraging/
- *North America (OH/KY) Field Guides? : r/foraging* https://www.reddit.com/r/foraging/comments/rfl9lh/north_america_ohky_field_guides/
- *A Beginners Guide to Foraging for Wild Edibles With Kids* https://wilderchild.com/blogs/news/foraging-for-wild-edibles-with-kids

- *Cloud Classification* https://www.weather.gov/lmk/cloud_classification
- *How to Choose Kids' Rain Gear* https://www.rei.com/learn/expert-advice/how-to-choose-kids-rain-gear.html
- *Survival Shelter Building Basics* https://survivaldispatch.com/survival-shelter-building-basics/
- *Thunderstorm Safety* https://www.redcross.org/get-help/how-to-prepare-for-emergencies/types-of-emergencies/thunderstorm.html
- *Cuts and scrapes: First aid* https://www.mayoclinic.org/first-aid/first-aid-cuts/basics/art-20056711
- *First Aid: Strains and Sprains (for Parents) |KidsHealth* https://kidshealth.org/en/parents/strains-sprains-sheet.html#:~:text=
- *First-Aid Kit (for Parents)* https://kidshealth.org/en/parents/firstaid-kit.html
- *What to Do About Bug Bites and Stings (for Parents)* https://kidshealth.org/en/parents/insect-stings-sheet.html
- *Animal Tracking with Kids: Beginners Guide* https://www.discoveringanew.com/blog-4/animal-tracking-with-kids
- *Bear Safety with kids! - Hey Bear* https://www.heybear.com/blogs/bear-education/bear-safety-with-kids
- *A Guide to Identify Venomous Snakes in North America* https://animal-care.com/blog/a-guide-to-identify-venomous-snakes-in-north-america/
- *32 Wilderness Survival Skills for Kids* https://thesurvivalmom.com/wilderness-survival-skills-kids/
- *Outdoor Skills: Teaching Kids How to Build A Fire* https://runwildmychild.com/building-fires-kids/
- *Survival Skills Challenge: Building a Shelter* https://theresjustonemommy.com/survival-skills-challenge-building-a-shelter/
- *Compass Treasure Hunt* https://learn.eartheasy.com/guides/compass-treasure-hunt/

- *How Outdoor Activities Build Resilience in Children*
  https://www.psychologytoday.com/us/blog/
  supporting-resilient-kids/202407/how-outdoor-
  activities-build-resilience-in-children#:~:text=*Why
  Family Outdoor Adventure Improved Mental Health* ...
  https://milkxwhiskey.com/blogs/wyldness-blog/
  why-family-outdoor-adventure-improved-mental-
  health-and-bonding-with-your-child
- *Top 10 Tips for Campfire Safety* https://www.
  reserveamerica.com/articles/camping/top-10-tips-
  for-campfire-safety/
- *33 Easy Camping Meals You Can Actually Make
  Outdoors* https://www.tasteofhome.com/collection/
  favorite-camping-recipes/
- *Survival Shelters: 15 Best Designs and How to Build
  Them* https://www.outdoorlife.com/survival-
  shelters-15-best-designs-wilderness-shelters/
- *Emergency Signaling: How to Get Rescued When* ...
  https://www.battlbox.com/blogs/battlbox/
  emergency-signaling-how-to-get-rescued-when-
  stranded-in-the-wild
- *Ways to Signal for Help in the Wilderness* https://www.
  fieldandstream.com/survival/ways-to-signal-for-
  help-in-the-wilderness
- *How To Make an Emergency Signal Fire - Live Fire Gear*
  https://www.livefiregear.com/blog/how-to-make-
  an-emergency-signal-fire/
- *32+ Survival Skills Your Child Should Know & Be Able to*
  ... https://thesurvivalmom.com/32-survival-skills-
  your-child-should-know-and-be-able-to-do-asap/
- *32+ Survival Skills Your Child Should Know & Be Able to*
  ... https://thesurvivalmom.com/32-survival-skills-
  your-child-should-know-and-be-able-to-do-asap/
- *Desert Habitat* https://kids.nationalgeographic.com/
  nature/habitats/article/desert
- *Learning to Navigate - Discover the Forest* https://
  discovertheforest.org/activites/learning-
  navigate#:~:text=*Survival 101 | Weird But True! | S1 E7*

| *Full Episode ...* https://www.youtube.com/watch?v=YgUUDxqETck

- *32 Wilderness Survival Skills for Kids* https://thesurvivalmom.com/wilderness-survival-skills-kids/
- *30 Survival Skills Activities for Kids* https://www.educatorstechnology.com/2023/06/30-survival-skills-activities-for-kids.html
- *Wilderness Survival Priority 1: STOP - Troop 116* https://scouttroop116.com/Survival-1-STOP.html

Made in the USA
Monee, IL
30 November 2024

71826570R00083